PIKE'S VENGEANCE

Colorado Territory Series Book II

JOHN LEGG

WOLFPACK
PUBLISHING
— EST 2013 —

WOLFPACK
PUBLISHING
— EST 2013 —

Pike's Vengeance

Paperback Edition
Copyright © 2021 John Legg

This book is a work of fiction. Any references to historical events,
real people or real places are used fictitiously. Other names, charac-
ters, places and events are products of the author's imagination, and
any resemblance to actual events, places or persons, living or dead,
is entirely coincidental.

All rights reserved. No part of this book may be reproduced by any
means without the prior written consent of the publisher, other
than brief quotes for reviews.

Wolfpack Publishing
5130 S. Fort Apache Road, 215-380
Las Vegas, NV 89148

wolfpackpublishing.com

Paperback ISBN: 978-1-64734-293-7
eBook ISBN: 978-1-64734-292-0

PIKE'S VENGEANCE

CHAPTER 1

"A word with you, Mr. Pike."

"What can I do for you, Marshal?"

"Come along with me peaceably." He waggled his pistol just a bit to make sure Pike noticed.

Brodie Pike had seen it and was not too concerned. "And why would I do that?"

"You're under arrest in the killin' of Harry Tilford."

"What makes you think I killed him?"

"You were the last one seen with him."

"That can't be."

"Oh?"

"I wasn't the last person to see him or, hell, even the next to last. I never met the man. Wouldn't know him if I fell over him."

"We'll let a judge and jury decide that. Now hand me those revolvers and come along."

"I ain't givin' up my pistols with that bunch over there watchin' us."

Marshal Milt Yeager glanced across the street, then looked back at Pike. "I did a little checkin' on you, Mr. Pike. Seems like you're a damn good bounty hunter."

"I am," Pike said with confidence, not boasting.

"I also heard you ain't known for killin' men unnecessarily."

"That's true, too. I don't relish killin'."

"And it seems like you're an honest man."

Pike smiled a bit. "I try to be, as much as a man can be in my profession."

"This may seem foolish, but I'm of a mind that you are innocent of this."

"I am."

"I still have to arrest you and let the court figure out if that's true."

"Reckon I can understand that."

"You'll come along without a fuss?"

"Long's I can keep my pistols 'til we get to the jail. I won't cause no trouble unless one of those mouse turds starts it."

Yeager stared at him a few moments, then nodded. He slid his own pistol away. "Let's go then."

Both men kept a wary eye on the group of maybe six men moving with them on the other side of the street. When Marshal Yeager and Pike entered the lawman's office, Yeager said, "I'll take those pistols now, Mr. Pike."

The bounty hunter stared at Yeager for a moment. He liked what he saw—an honest, hardworking lawman who took his job seriously. Pike undid his gun belt and handed it over.

Yeager looked at the holstered revolvers, then at Pike. "You mind if I look at them?" he asked.

Pike was torn. He did not like anyone touching his weapons. It was like he was being asked to bare himself in public. He drew a deep breath, let it out, then nodded. He was pleased to see that Yeager eased one of the six-guns out almost reverently.

"Damn, this thing is one fine piece of weaponry." There was nothing special about its look and no special engraving, just a regular blued barrel and worn though well-cared-for walnut stocks. However, the balance and the ease with which it settled in the hand was superb. "This a Colt? It looks a little different."

"A Colt .44. Had it converted from cap and ball a few years ago."

Yeager slid it gently back into the holster and did not bother to look at the other. It would be, he knew, of the same quality and as well cared for as the first. He looked at Pike again. "I know that was asking a lot of you, Mr. Pike, but I thank you for allowing it. It ain't often a man like me gets to hold such a special piece of gun work."

Pike relaxed. "Order a couple, then find yourself a good gunsmith. I bet you could have a pair just like 'em, fitted just for your hand." He smiled a little.

"Would be nice," Yeager said wistfully, knowing it could never happen. He sighed. "All right, Mr. Pike, much as I might dislike it, I got to put you in the back."

Without a word, Pike headed toward the cells. He stretched out on the cold iron cot, covered only by a thin blanket, and closed his eyes. There was no use worrying about things now. He would wait to see what happened before deciding what to do.

By the time Deputy Jonah North brought Pike a meal several hours later, the bounty hunter was annoyed. "Sounds like things're gettin' a might rambunctious outside," he said.

"It sure as hell is. Mob's grown larger and nastier."

"Marshal Yeager and you and Deputy Runkles got your hands full, I reckon."

"Just me and Milt. Earl ain't nowhere to be found."

"Just skedaddled, eh?"

"Seems like."

"You and the marshal able to handle things?"

"Be honest, I got my doubts. That mob seems mighty determined to see you dancin' at the end of a rope."

"Reckon someone in Arrowhead took a strong dislike to me for some reason. Can't figure out why, though."

"Maybe for killin' Harry Tilford."

"Like I told Marshal Yeager, I didn't kill him or no one else in Arrowhead."

"Marshal seems to think you're tellin' the truth."

"I am."

North grinned. "I believe you too."

"You and the marshal need help with that bunch?"

"You?" When Pike nodded, he said, "You'd be a good one to have on our side, but I figure it'd cause even more trouble."

"Reckon you're right. But it's my neck they want to stretch, and if I can keep it out of a noose, I'll be damned glad to help out."

"I'll keep it in mind."

As the day wore on, Pike became more concerned. He wasn't afraid, but he did not like being unarmed and caged with only two men between him and a mob bent on lynching him.

Late in the afternoon, Marshal Yeager came back to the office. When he opened the front door, the noise from the crowd outside rushed in at Pike. The lawman looked tired and tense when he stopped in front of the cell. He had Pike's gun belt in one hand and the cell key in the other.

"About time you come to give me my guns back so I can help you and Deputy North."

"Like Jonah told you, that'd just worsen the trouble."

"So why're you here with my guns?"

"I'm gonna give 'em back to you and let you go."

"That ought to be interestin', Marshal. Ain't but the one door."

Yeager unlocked the cell door and handed Pike his Colts. "Hope you're good at climbin'."

Pike stared at him in befuddlement as he hooked on his gun belt. Then he followed Yeager to the last cell to the left.

Yeager pointed at the ceiling. "Big tree fell on it a few weeks ago. Ain't had time to properly fix it, just laid a couple boards over the hole and covered it with canvas to keep the weather out. Roof ain't that high. Put a chair on the bunk, and you should be able to shove the boards out of the way and haul yourself up through the hole."

"Reckon I can."

"Once you get up there, drop down out back. Head

across Feather Street and back around Schmidt's saddle shop and down Fourth Street to Pony's livery. Grab your horse and hightail it out of Arrowhead. I suggest you don't come back, at least not for a spell."

"What about you and Deputy North?"

"Ain't your concern."

"But it's my neck ..."

"Don't matter. I don't have the time or patience for discussin' it with you. I'm the law here, and it's my job to keep the peace. That includes calmin' down a bunch of drunken thugs lookin' to hang an innocent man. I take my job seriously, Mr. Pike. Might seem foolish to some, but not to me."

"Nor to me, Marshal ... Milt." He paused, then, "You certain about this?"

"I am."

Pike grinned sadly. "You are a damn fool, Milt. Most brave men—heroes—are."

"Adiós, Mr. Pike. Don't break your neck when you jump down." The lawman hurried toward the front.

Pike waited only a moment before stacking a chair atop the iron bunk. After he climbed atop it, he shoved the boards out of the way. It took only a minute more to pull himself up onto the roof. He dangled off by his fingers, then dropped to the street and hurried off, figuring that with all the commotion in front of the marshal's office, getting into the hotel where he had been staying would be easy. He was not about to leave his saddlebags, Winchester, and the special rifle he carried with him behind.

He was right. He slipped up the stairs after entering the hotel through the door in the rear. In minutes, he had all his belongings and was heading down the street again. Before long, he slipped into the livery.

As Pike threw the saddle blanket on his horse, he heard someone approach. He swung around, keeping the animal between him and whoever was coming, slipped out a pistol, and rested his gun hand across the horse's back.

"No need to shoot me, Mr. Pike," said Pony Stallings, the liveryman.

"Why not?"

"I ain't your enemy."

"You sure?"

"If I was aimin' to be in on the lynchin', I'd be out there with that rabble. 'Sides, I agree with Marshal Yeager."

"Think I'm innocent, do you?"

"Yep. Certain of it."

"Why's that?"

"I'm pretty sure I know who done it."

"Who?"

"Drew Bidwell."

"Who's he?"

"Son of a bitch leadin' that batch of no-accounts out there."

Pike slid his pistol away and grabbed his saddle from where it sat on the stall divider. "Why do you think he killed Tilford?"

"Tilford whupped his ass in cards yesterday. Way I heard it, Bidwell had a top-notch hand, almost a certain winner, but he didn't have any cash left. He asked Tilford if he could use his pocket watch to cover the bet. Tilford said no, told Bidwell the watch wasn't worth enough. Bidwell had to fold with a full house. Tilford didn't have to show his hand, but he did—pair of fours—grinnin' from ear to ear. Bidwell was some angry then, boy."

"I would reckon so. But you don't play the game if you can't cover the bets."

"That's a fact. Bidwell come in the saloon later last night, with some blood on his shirt and one hand. Said he cut himself hackin' off some meat for his supper. They found Tilford's body this mornin', stabbed to death."

"Didn't anyone put together that Bidwell had blood on him and Tilford was found stabbed after havin' gloated about beatin' Bidwell with such a poor hand?"

"Sure. The marshal, Deputy North, and a few others."

"Includin' you?"

"Yep. I might be just a dumb ol' horse handler, but I ain't entirely a fool."

"I'd agree with that. But why didn't Milt arrest Bidwell?" Pike asked as he finished saddling and bridling his horse.

"Soon as word spread about Tilford's body bein' found. Bidwell started agitatin', throwin' his weight around, expoundin' on how it must be a stranger who done it."

"And I had told him yesterday at the saloon that he was botherin' me with all the shoutin' he was doin' almost right in my ear. Didn't know who he was at the time."

"Bull's-eye."

Pike slung his saddlebags on the horse and tied them down, then hooked on both scabbards. He climbed into the saddle.

"I suggest you get as far away from here as fast as you can, Mr. Pike."

"You ain't the first to tell me that."

"Reckon I wasn't, but it makes sense."

Pike sighed in annoyance. This didn't sit well with him, but it seemed the smartest thing to do. "Thanks, Mr. Stallings. I'm obliged."

CHAPTER 2

The roar of gunfire from outside the marshal's office boomed up the street to the livery. Pike and Stallings stared in that direction. Though it was dusk, the lantern light in front of the lawman's office allowed them to see Marshal Yeager and Deputy North fall, as did a couple of the men in the mob.

"Ah, sweet Jesus," Pike growled in rage. He went to ram his heels into the horse's sides, but Stallings grabbed his reins and jerked hard.

"No!" he snapped.

"Let go, Pony, or I'll kill you here and now."

"Don't be a fool, Pike."

"Dammit, the marshal needs my help."

"Not now he don't. He's dead, sure as hell. So's North. Getting' yourself killed—and that's what'll happen if you go down there now—won't help nobody."

"It's my fault, dammit all."

"No, it ain't. It's Bidwell's fault, and that herd of ruffians with him. Milt was doin' his duty. He knew it could come to a bad end, but that's what he was hired for, and he'd be mighty angry if you were to get yourself killed now after he got you out of that jail. Even if he is dead. His ghost'd hound you for all eternity for bein' so foolish."

Pike sat there on his horse, seething at the senseless death of a good man and his own helplessness at being unable to do anything to change that. Slowly, the realization that Stallings was right began to settle on him. He closed his eyes for a moment and took a couple of deep breaths to ease the rage.

The shooting had stopped. Two men hurried into the jail and came out a few seconds later. "He's gone!" one of them yelled. But there was no one to hear him. The mob had scattered.

"You best be on your way, Mr. Pike," Stallings said, still holding the reins.

"Does Bidwell have any cronies he's close to?"

"Why do you want to know?" Stallings asked suspiciously.

"Just answer me."

Stallings looked up at Pike and nodded, smiling inwardly. He knew what the bounty hunter was planning. "Woody Gibbs. Short, powerful, mean as hell. Dunk Yost. Tall, skinny, ugly son of a bitch. Ain't too smart, but he's mean as a snake. Mel Jenks. Medium height, but real scrawny. Lurches instead of walks. Scar across his forehead. Claims some Comanches tried to scalp him but he killed 'em. He's full of mule crap. Ross Moss. Big as a small house, dumb as an outhouse. Follows Bidwell like a puppy. Don't cause trouble on his own, but he'll do whatever

Bidwell tells him to. You've seen Bidwell."

"That all?

"One other: Deputy Runkles."

"No wonder he wasn't around to help Milt and Jonah. Why didn't Milt fire him?"

"Earl's new at the job and didn't start associatin' with Bidwell 'til recent-like. Reckon he really didn't know."

"Thanks, Pony."

"I figure I know what you're planning, but I'd advise against it. Was I you, I'd hightail it for somewhere a long way off and keep movin'."

"Ain't my way, Pony."

"I figured that, too." He smiled, which Pike thought was a bit odd. "Would be nice to have some justice for Milt and Jonah."

Pike smiled back grimly. "Would be." He reached into a pocket and pulled out some coins, then handed Stallings three gold double eagles. "One of them's for you for takin' good care of my horse. The other two are for makin' sure Milt and Jonah get a top-notch burial."

"That ain't necessary. Milt's well-liked, and most people in town'll be happy to give him a right proper sendoff."

"Then give the money to their widows or mothers or something." He smiled again, a more pleasant one. "Just make sure you don't keep it all for yourself."

"You just stabbed me in the heart, Mr. Pike," Stallings said with a forced chuckle. "You need anything, you come to me however you can. Milt and Jonah were good men, honest and serious about their work. It's a goddamn sin what happened to 'em."

Pike nodded and stuck out his hand. Stallings shook it and let go of the reins. Pike trotted out of the barn, turned left, and headed south out of Arrowhead.

** ** ** ** **

Pike rapped on the back door of Pony Stallings' house two nights later. He got no response, and the light was extinguished. "C'mon, Pony, open up. It's Brodie Pike."

The light inside went back on, and the door opened. "What're you doin' here?" the liveryman asked as Pike stepped inside.

"I was takin' a moonlight stroll and thought I'd pay you a social visit." He plunked down at the table.

"Well, I sure am some pleased, I tell you," Stallings said flatly. "Coffee? Or some tanglefoot?"

"Coffee." Pike grinned. "With a dollop of tanglefoot."

Stallings supplied it, then sat across from Pike. "So, to what do I owe the pleasure of your company?"

"Need some supplies."

"Like what?"

"Small coffeepot and a fry pan. Coffee, bacon, beans, a bit of sugar and salt, maybe a few airtights. Not too much. I don't want to be draggin' a pack mule around. Enough for two, three days." He paused. "And some rope."

"Rope?" Stallings asked, staring at him with an expectant look. "What kind and how much?"

"I think you can figure that out."

"I reckon I can," Stallings replied with a sly grin.

"When do you want it?"

"Soon. I'll stop by again tomorrow night."

"Hell, stay here, Brodie. Plenty of room with Bessie gone to her reward."

"Nope. I'm responsible for enough death. I don't want the blood of another innocent man in Arrowhead on my hands."

"But you ain't ..."

Pike held up a hand to stop his companion. "You can say whatever you want, Pony, but you know damn well if it weren't for me, Milt and Jonah'd still be alive."

Stallings nodded. "Might be dangerous to come 'round here again tomorrow night."

"I did all right tonight. Likely I'll be able to do so tomorrow."

"But tonight, you ain't carryin' saddlebags full of stuff that might be noisy and maybe attract some unwanted attention."

"I ain't worried, but if you got another suggestion, I'll listen."

"I have a couple fellers who watch over some horses in pastures out of town a ways. I take supplies out to 'em now and again. I can make out that what I'm gonna do so. Might even bring 'em some, too, so nobody'll notice. I can leave the supplies somewhere you can find 'em easy."

"Like where?"

"A couple miles northeast of town, you'll find a stream, Bow Creek. Comes out of a small clump of boulders. Follow it for near half a mile. The creek splits, then joins back together maybe ten yards away. There's a little island there with a single fair-size cottonwood. I'll leave your supplies there under a tarp. You can get 'em whenever you want."

Pike thought it over for a few moments, then nodded. "That's what we'll do then. Obliged, Pony."

"You can bring some justice in this, no thanks're needed."

Pike pulled out some more coins and fingered out a double eagle. When he held it out to Stallings, the liveryman shook his head. "You give me more than enough the other day for takin' care of your horse for so short a time. I don't need no more for this."

"You certain?"

"I am."

** ** ** ** **

Pike leaned against a boulder atop a steep, rocky slope overlooking a pine-studded meadow that faded into a wide stand of aspens. Though he had been there since shortly after sunrise, he showed no signs of tiredness or boredom. He let his mind wander as his eyes watched the landscape.

Considering how enraged he still was about the deaths of Marshal Milt Yeager and Deputy Jonah North, his thoughts were mostly dark. Like the time he ran down Micah Parker and his gang after they had killed an eight-year-old girl during a train robbery because she screamed in fright. Or the time he took down the Ostling brothers when they ...

A wagon coming out of the aspens and starting across the meadow brought a halt to his reminiscing. Within moments, he could tell it was Pony Stallings, and his trajectory would bring him to the little island in the stream that ran behind the other side of the stony mound Pike was standing on.

Stallings was about halfway across the meadow when Pike spotted movement at the edge of the trees the liveryman had just left. Moments later, a man on horseback inched out from the aspens. Pike pulled out his telescoping spyglass and looked. Stallings' description of Dunk Yost—a tall, skinny, ugly son of a bitch—was pretty brief, but Pike was certain he was looking at the man. There were two reasons Pike could think of why Yost was out here, neither of them good. Either way, this was a situation that could not go unresolved.

Pike collapsed the telescope and put it back in the saddlebag, then pulled the .52-caliber Sharps sniper rifle with the full copper scope he had used in the Civil War from the special scabbard on the horse.

Stallings had moved out of Pike's sight before Yost began riding slowly across the meadow. The bounty hunter waited until Yost was less than a hundred yards away, then laid the Sharps across the boulder, sighted, and fired. Yost reeled in his saddle for a moment before toppling to the ground as the gunshot echoed off the mountains.

"Come on out of those trees, Pony!" Pike bellowed.

The wiry liveryman walked warily out onto the grass, saw Yost's horse, and stopped uncertainly. "Brodie?" he shouted.

"Up here." When Stallings looked up the hill at him, Pike asked, "Where's your wagon?"

"Back in the trees."

"Why didn't you come out with it?"

"You try turnin' the damn thing around in there." Annoyance was strong in his voice. "What in hell's gotten into you?"

Pike said nothing as he slid the Sharps back into its special scabbard and walked down the rocky slope, leading the horse. When he was on level ground, he jerked his head toward Yost's horse and walked that way. When they got there, Pike pointed. "Friend of yours?"

"Ain't no friend of mine. It's Dunk Yost." His eyes tightened. "What in hell's goin' on, Brodie?"

"He was followin' you, so I took him out."

"Good. Son of a bitch deserved it. But you're actin' like I had something to do with it."

"Did you?"

"You got something to say to me, Mr. Pike, come out and say it. Far's as I know, you ain't so shy a fellow to keep an accusation to himself."

"I figure there was two reasons he was followin' you, neither of 'em good and both involvin' me."

"And what're those two reasons?"

"One, he was followin' you without you knowin' about it, hopin' you'd lead him to me."

"The other?" Stallings asked, suspicion thick in his voice.

"That you were leadin' him to me on purpose, and he was hangin' back, not wantin' to let me see him if I was around."

"Ain't true," Stallings said with a shrug. "But now that you've shot him dead, he can't tell you that, now, can he?"

"That's a fact." Pike grinned. "Either you're tellin' me the truth, or you should be on the stage with those Shakespeare actors roamin' around."

"You are one exasperatin' fellow, Mr. Pike."

"I expect I am."

"Why the hell would he be followin' me? He had no reason to."

"When Milt let me go, I needed a horse to head out of town. Since none was stolen, and mine was gone out of your stable ..."

"They didn't know where your horse was. Could've been in Berger's place down the road."

"I expect they had someone watchin' both places. You left with the wagon this mornin', so Yost followed you. I reckon that if Berger also left, someone would've followed him too."

"Damn." Stallings sighed. "Well, I'll go see if I can wrangle that wagon around so's we can throw Dunk's body in it."

"Ain't necessary. Just go on and put my supplies where you said you would and go about your business. I'll take care of this trash."

"I figure you'll give him a proper sendoff?" He smiled, but his eyes seemed to sparkle.

Pike nodded.

CHAPTER 3

Deputy Earl Runkles—now Marshal Earl Runkles—
was an early riser, and there were few people on the
streets of Arrowhead as he headed to the office. He
was surprised, therefore, when he saw a small but
growing crowd in front of the building. Angry, he
started shoving his way through the people. "Come
on, folks, let me through," he snapped. "What the
hell's gotten into all of you?" He stopped with one
foot on the wooden sidewalk and stared.

Propped upright against the door of his office was
the rigid body of Dunk Yost. It took a few moments
for the scene to drill itself into his mind, then he
roared, "Who the hell's responsible for this?" He
spun, looking from one face in the crowd to another.

No one said anything, though there were a few
snickers and chuckles.

"Dammit, somebody go get the undertaker."
When no one moved, he sputtered, "Bastards!" As
he pushed back through the crowd, he snapped,
"When I find the son of a bitch who did this,

there'll be hell to pay."

Leaning against the wall of a cobbler's shop across the street, Pony Stallings smiled slyly with a sense of satisfaction. He watched Runkles march angrily down the street, then turned and headed for his livery.

** ** ** ** **

It took five days, or rather, nights, but Pike finally knew where all of Drew Bidwell's men lived, where they ate, what saloons and whorehouses or cribs they frequented, and the hours they kept.

The next night, Pike rode into Arrowhead just after midnight. He kept off the main street, though he could see when he looked down the alleys that the town was pretty much deserted. Pike pulled up and tied his horse to the back corner of an empty warehouse. If it weren't for the half-moon and a batch of stars, it would be pitch-black.

He patted his horse on the neck, then headed down the dirt path that ran between the backs of several buildings and the river. He stopped at the back door of the Clarion Hotel, a different lodging house from the one he had stayed at. The door led into the hotel's kitchen, which had closed hours ago for the night. The door was locked, but it only took a few moments for Pike to jimmy it open with his Bowie.

He slipped through the deserted kitchen and the empty dining room. At the far end, he stopped and looked into the lobby. The clerk was sleeping quietly in an upholstered chair in a corner behind the desk.

Silently, he headed up the stairs to the second floor, then to the room at the end of the hall on the left. Pike didn't think Woody Gibbs would lock his room, and he was right.

Like a ghost, Pike entered the room and paused, leaning back against the door. Gibbs snored heavily. The moon and stars cast their feeble light through the window. It was enough, barely, for Pike to see that Gibbs was alone. There was a coal-oil lamp on a table near the window, and Pike decided to take the chance. He lit it, keeping the flame very low, then picked it up with one hand and rested his other on the butt of one Colt. There had been no change in Gibbs' breathing.

Pike set the lantern on a small table next to the bed and raised the flame a little. Gibbs shifted a bit but did not wake. Pike pulled the pistol with his left hand and the big Bowie with his right and rested the latter lightly on Gibbs' throat. Then he stuck the muzzle of the pistol in Gibbs' ear and thumbed back the hammer.

Gibbs started and was ready to reach for his holstered six-shooter, which was hanging from the bedpost, but he froze when he felt the knife blade at his throat.

"Mornin', Mr. Gibbs," Pike said, making no effort to make it sound pleasant. He moved the pistol back a couple of inches.

Aware that the blade was close to his jugular and was just barely breaking the skin, Gibbs eased his head around. His eyes widened. "You!" he whispered.

"In the flesh."

"What're you doin' here?" The fright in his eyes faded a little.

"I reckon you can figure that out."

"You ain't gonna kill me," the man said, feeling more confident. He tensed, preparing to take out Pike. "You were gonna do that, you would've done it already."

"You sure?"

"Yep." Gibbs tried to smile insolently, but it didn't work.

"You're wrong, Mr. Gibbs. Only reason I haven't done so is that I wanted you to see your executioner."

"Just who the ..." Gibbs' words turned into a strangled gurgle as Pike's razor-sharp blade easily slid deep into his throat.

Pike jerked his arm back, managing to avoid most of the blood fountain that resulted.

Gibbs jerked and thrashed, trying to do something, anything, to live, but in less than a minute, he was still and the blood had slowed to a trickle. Pike swiftly pulled off the rope coiled around his shoulder and shook out the lasso. Grabbing Gibbs' hair, he jerked the man's upper body up, worked the loop around the torso under his arms, and pulled it tight. He let the body fall back onto the bed.

Pike stood still for a few moments, listening, but there was no sound of anyone moving around in the hotel. He went and opened the door to the balcony. He returned to the bed and eased Gibbs' body off it, then dragged it outside onto the balcony. He tossed the end of the rope over the railing and pulled it back through the space between two slats. He estimated the length, then tied the rope to the thick log used to hold up the balcony's roof.

Before he could do anything else, he slipped back into the shadows as two riders passed in front of the hotel. Neither looked up. Pike waited until they were out of sight, then lifted Gibbs' body and dropped it over the railing, hoping the log would hold. It did. Gibbs' body bounced a few times, then hung there, swaying a little, his feet two yards from the ground.

With a grim smile, Pike went back inside, shut the door, blew out the lantern, and left. He went out the same way he had entered. The clerk was still sleeping. Five minutes later, he was riding out of town.

** ** ** ** **

Pike stood on a rocky outcrop and watched as Pony Stallings drove his old wagon across the meadow toward Pike's original camp. He waited long enough to be fairly certain no one was following the liveryman, then mounted his horse and rode down to meet him.

Stallings spotted him and pulled the wagon to a halt. "Thought I'd bring you some supplies. It's been a while since you came callin'." He grinned at his little joke, then pointed at Pike's sleeve. "Good thing I brought you a new shirt. It's in one of the sacks. I was gonna leave everything at the same spot."

"Obliged. I've moved my camp."

"Don't trust me?" Stallings asked with a gimlet eye.

"Don't trust the folks who killed Marshal Yeager and Deputy North."

"Good thinkin'. I don't know if anyone in town suspects you, but you sure got them folks riled up, especially after takin' care of Woody Gibbs the way you did. Made a real impression on the town."

"Reckon it did."

"So, where do ya want me to put these supplies?"

"How much you have?"

"Couple sacks, not too big, not too small."

"Can I carry 'em on my horse?"

"Reckon so, but I'd not go too far, though you do have a mighty strong animal."

"She is, but I don't abuse her any either."

"That's a fact. I could tell that right off when you brought her to my stables the first time." Stallings climbed off the wagon, tied the two sacks together, and hung them over the back of Pike's horse, sliding the rope between the cantle and Pike's bedroll, where they hung over the saddlebags.

"Gonna be hard to top killin' Gibbs," Stallings said as he climbed back into his wagon. "What've you got planned for the next one?"

Pike just stared at him.

"Right. Damn-fool question. See ya next time, whenever that'll be."

Pike watched silently as Stallings turned the wagon in a wide, slow circle and pulled out. The liveryman's last question bothered him for some reason other than it being a stupid question, and he thought it unusual that Stallings had brought him a new shirt. He couldn't figure out why Stallings would think he needed one, other than that it was obvious Gibbs' neck had been slit. Pike had had a fresh shirt, which he was wearing, and he had tossed the old one down a crack between some rocks.

It seemed curious, but he put those thoughts out of his mind for now.

He continued watching until Stallings had crested the slight hump of the hill half a mile away, then turned his horse and rode into the woods to his new campsite. It was under an overhang on a slope hard up against a cliff.

He unloaded his supplies, then built a small fire. He set a couple of the ham slices Stallings had brought in a frying pan over the fire, then filled the coffeepot with water, pounded up beans in a rawhide sack with a rock, dumped those in the pot, and set that in the fire too. As he waited, he began questioning what he had been doing. Well, not so much what he had been doing but whether to continue. He was tired of killing, and to most people, what he had done would have been ample payback for the ruthless murder of the two lawmen. He finally sighed in resignation. He had taken on a chore, and no matter how distasteful it had become, he would finish it. No one with any sense would fault him for riding out—except himself. To do so would go against his grain, even though if his history was any guide, something might very well go very wrong.

As he reached for the food, he hesitated, wondering if the ham was poisoned, but he realized he was being foolish. While something about Pony Stallings had begun to bother him, he didn't think the liveryman would try to kill him. Even if Stallings was up to no good, he would want the bounty hunter to finish the job. Pike carefully pulled the frying pan out of the fire and began cutting up the ham. While letting it cool for a moment, he poured a mug of coffee, then, with a devil may care attitude, dug in. As he'd figured, there was nothing wrong with the ham or the coffee.

Finally settling back, he pondered what to do next. He could come up with no concrete plan. He figured he'd just finish his gruesome tasks and be on his way. He had had enough of Arrowhead and New Mexico Territory.

He waited two days before heading into town again, and when he did, it was during a heavy rainstorm. Despite his wide-brimmed Stetson and good slicker, he was not happy to be roaming about in such weather, but he knew that it would give him good cover. Most everyone would be inside on a night like this. Of course, the other side of that was it might be difficult to find his quarry. It did help that he knew which saloons Mel Jenks and Ross Moss frequented. He hoped he could catch them together.

He left his horse in an alley, strolled to Main Street, and waited inside the recessed doorway of the hardware store while he watched the Rotting Pig saloon. Luck had shifted to favor him for a change, and the enormous Moss shuffled out of the tavern less than fifteen minutes after Pike had started watching.

An idea popped into Pike's head, and he trotted to the alley where he had left his horse as Moss lumbered down the street on the wooden sidewalk.

Pike mounted, slipped the coiled rope from where it hung on the saddle, shook it out, and headed into the main street. He followed Moss slowly until the obese man went to cross the street between buildings. Pike moved swiftly alongside Moss, who looked up, surprised. Pike dropped the loop over the man's head and yanked it tight around his neck, cutting off any exclamation.

Before Moss could react, Pike spurred his horse into a trot, jerking Moss off his feet and dragging him through the mud. He stopped under the big oak in the center of town, then tossed the loose end of the rope over a stout branch, looped the end around his saddle horn, and backed the horse up. Moss was lifted high into the air, kicking and trying to scream, but he could not. So intent was he on trying to claw the rope from around his neck that he forgot the revolver hanging in a sagging holster around his lard-encased waist.

Pike got the horse as close to a hitching rail as he could, then dismounted, tied the rope to the rail, and unwound it from the saddle horn. Moss dropped some, but his feet remained a foot or so off the ground. He was still struggling to escape the rope as he swung in the rain.

Pike remounted his horse, paying little attention to Moss, whose weight kept the rope tight around his throat, not allowing his hands any room to pull it away as he slowly strangled to death. He did shuffle the horse over close enough to take out Moss' six-gun and toss it in the mud. With no sense of joy or even satisfaction, Pike rode off.

He didn't get far. He couldn't believe his luck was holding when he spotted Mel Jenks stumbling out of a nearby alley where the cribs of the cheaper prostitutes were. "I'll be dammed," he muttered.

He spun his horse and raced back to the hardware store where he had started his vigil. He quickly punched a hole in the glass of the door, having no fear of being heard with the rain and its accompanying thunder, and opened it, then ran inside and snatched another coil of rope, as well as a hickory ax handle. He was outside and on his horse again, ax handle in hand, coiled rope hanging from the saddle horn, in less than two minutes.

Jenks was standing under the oak, dumbfounded, staring at the swinging corpse of his pal Ross Moss. Given the storm's noise, he was unaware of Pike stopping just behind him and sliding off his horse.

Pike stepped up and slammed Jenks across the lower back with the hickory handle. To his surprise, the scrawny man sagged but did not fall. Though drunk, he managed to spin, although he slipped in the mud, making Pike's next swing of the ax handle miss. He surged up and slammed a shoulder into Pike's middle, driving him back and almost knocking him down, but the bounty hunter managed to keep his footing on the slick ground, though he dropped the ax handle. Pike smashed a forearm across Jenks' nose, breaking it, but Jenks was stronger than Pike had figured and managed to get in a few punches, hurting Pike but doing little damage.

Pike regained his equilibrium, and as Jenks reached for his six-shooter, he punched the skinny man twice. Jenks wavered, then fell into the muck. Pike kicked him in the side and then the forehead, then booted the revolver away. Pike staggered back, breathing heavily, and saw that Jenks was out of commission, at least for a few seconds.

Swiftly forming a makeshift noose, Pike slipped it over Jenks' head, tossed the other end over another branch of the oak, hoisted Jenks up as he had Moss, and tied the rope to the same hitching rail. It was a much easier task this time because of Jenks' considerably slighter build.

The bounty hunter mounted his horse and looked at the stringy killer, whose struggles were already lessening. "Killin' a good lawman doesn't sit well with some folks, and payment comes hard, boys."

He rode out of Arrowhead with the storm still battering the town. With him rode a sense of unease. He didn't mind wreaking vengeance on these heartless men, but he was beginning to feel that something was wrong and he was being played for a fool. It had happened before more times than he liked to admit, and he was afraid it was happening again, though he didn't know how or why.

CHAPTER 4

Pike decided it was time to finish it. He planned to take out Drew Bidwell, the ostensible leader of the killers, first and leave Deputy Earl Runkles for last, considering that the killing of a lawman—another lawman—might raise another ruckus. Then he planned to leave this godforsaken town and never return. He thought he had left a large enough message for the people of Arrowhead. The killings of Bidwell and Runkles would be straightforward.

The kernel of suspicion regarding Pony Stallings had him revising his plans. He would track down Runkles first and try to get the truth of whether Bidwell was really the leader of the killers or if Stallings had deceived him.

First, however, he moved his small camp to a spot alongside a rivulet on the mountain on the eastern side of the town instead of the northern end, where he had been all along. Something niggled at his mind, making him even more cautious than usual.

Once that was done, he spent several nights

prowling Arrowhead, checking on Bidwell and Runkles, learning their habits. He supposed he could have just shot them from ambush and been done with it, but that went against his grain. The others had had to face him, excerpt Dunk Yost, and he wanted the main killer and the deputy to do the same.

He also kept an eye on Stallings, who Pike saw talking with Runkles at one point. It seemed like a friendly conversation, which bothered the bounty hunter. It could have been innocent, with Stallings playing up to the deputy to keep on his good side. It also could be more sinister.

It also concerned Pike that he had never seen Bidwell and Runkles together. He knew that might be because he was not around in the daytime. Also, at first glance, Bidwell didn't seem likely to be a killer. Drew Bidwell was a medium-size fellow with a pasty white face partly hidden by a wispy beard and thin blondish muttonchops. He always wore a conservative suit and a derby. From what Pike had seen, Bidwell appeared to be a stable family man. He was not rich, but he owned a prosperous watchmaking and jewelry shop. He ate in the better restaurants, though not at the top level, and he drank at one of the more upscale saloons. It just didn't seem to Pike that Bidwell would stab a man to death over losing a poker hand. Not that any of that meant much. The bounty hunter had met killers who looked as unprepossessing as Bidwell. For the time being, Pike put it out of his mind as best he could.

Almost a week after he had killed Moss and Jenks,

he slipped into town early one evening. It was dark enough for him to hide in the shadows but early enough that there were a considerable number of people about. He stopped at the corner of the jailhouse, at the end of a small street, and waited in the shadows. From his surveillance, he knew Runkles would be ending his rounds at about this time and returning to the office.

Sure enough, Runkles appeared minutes later. As the deputy started opening the office door, Pike slipped behind him and shoved him through it. Runkles stumbled into the desk. With a hand on the top, he tried to push himself up and around and reach for a pistol.

Pike punched him on the side of the face, and Runkles fell. He then stomped on the deputy's stomach, leaving him gasping for air. Pike grabbed Runkles' revolver and tossed it away, then grabbed him by the shirtfront and dragged him, weakly kicking and squirming, toward the cells in back and dropped him in one. He went back, locked the front door, and pulled down the curtain. He didn't expect anyone to show up, but that was the way Runkles usually left the office at this hour.

He fired up a lantern and returned to the back with a set of handcuffs, which he used to hook Runkles' left arm to the bars of the cell, allowing the deputy to stand but not sit. Runkles, having regained his breath, started to complain, but Pike waggled a finger at him.

"You will have your opportunity to speak in just a moment, boy. Protestin' will do you no good anyway. You are where you are, and there you will stay 'til I say otherwise." He let that sink in, then asked, "Who's your boss?" When Runkles remained close-mouthed, Pike said, "Now is the time for you to speak, boy."

"The mayor," Runkles said with a smirk.

"A poor attitude accompanied by lies would be mighty poor choices when it comes to your health."

"You gonna shoot me?" Runkles was still sneering.

"I could do that, but it would be very loud in this small space and might hurt my ears. Can't have that. Still, I got me this here big pig-sticker, as well as my fists and boots. I reckon they could cause some serious damage."

"You think you can scare me with those foolish threats?" Runkles' cockiness had slipped a little.

Pike smashed a fist into the deputy's face, shattering his nose and staggering him. He would have fallen but for the handcuffs allowing him only to sag. Runkles managed to pull himself back up, and with his free hand, he wiped at the blood pouring from his nose.

"That answer your question, boy?"

"Maybe," Runkles mumbled. "But I could yell for help. That'd bring some people runnin'."

"Doubt it. I don't think anyone'd hear you, and I don't think anyone'd give a damn that you were in trouble. And if anyone was foolish enough to try to help you, you'd be dead before they got in the door, and they'd be dead moments later. And unless there was a passel of 'em, I'd be out of Arrowhead before anyone knew who was responsible."

"You seem mighty damn sure of yourself."

"In this case, I am. Now, who killed that fellow Tilford?"

"Why should I talk to you? You'll just kill me when I spill what I know."

"True, I could. But unlike some fellas, I don't generally cotton to killin' lawmen, even pretend ones like you. You tell me what you know, and I'll finish my business here and be gone. So, who killed Tilford?"

Runkles hesitated a moment as if deciding whether to answer, then sighed in resignation and said, "Woody Gibbs."

"Not Drew Bidwell?"

"Nope. That soft old fart wouldn't hurt a fly. Besides, he and Harry were the best of friends. Even if he was given to use violence, he wouldn't have killed Harry. Not over a lousy bet. They often ribbed each other when winnin' big, maybe even complained loudly to others about losin', but they'd always be good pals the next day."

"Why'd Gibbs do it?" Pike was not surprised.

"He was told to."

"By who?"

"Pony Stallings."

Pike was a bit more surprised. "Why?"

"Way I heard it was that Bidwell and Tilford cheated Pony in a business dealing some time back. He's hated them ever since. When he saw that Tilford won big and Bidwell was angry—he'd been drinkin', though it wouldn't have mattered in the mornin'—Pony saw his chance. It was easier because you were in town."

"A stranger carryin' a gun?"

"Yep."

"But Tilford was knifed to death, not shot."

"Most folks didn't know that. The marshal did, of course, but he had a mob formin' and decided to get you into jail."

"Almost makes sense."

"Woody took the money Harry had won, so it looked like a robbery. Pony figured he and the others would raise a ruckus and you'd be blamed."

"Worked to a point. It wasn't for Marshal Yeager, I'd have been dead weeks ago."

"That was the idea. But the damn fool let you go." He paused. "Mind if I ask you something?"

"Go ahead," Pike said with a shrug.

"You killed Woody and the others, didn't you?" When Pike nodded, he added, "Why?"

"Revenge for them killing Marshal Yeager and Deputy North."

"How'd you know they were responsible?"

"I was told."

"By Pony?"

"Of course. But now I can't understand why. If they were helpin' him in all this, why have me kill 'em?"

"You'll have to ask him that. I ain't tellin' you no more. I told you too much already. Now let me go. I'll stay here 'til mornin' before I spread the alarm." He looked hopeful and doubtful at the same time. He was beginning to regret having said anything, but he knew he'd had no choice and now hoped Pike would keep his word.

Pike's stomach knotted as the knowledge that he had been duped ate at him. It did not matter that the men he'd killed had deserved it for the reason he had done it and probably more, but it disgusted him that it had been someone else's decision, not his. Finally, he rose and headed out of the cell.

"Hey, where're you goin'? Come back here and let me loose, dammit."

"Just hold your horses. I gotta get the key." He grabbed Runkles' Colt from the floor and stuffed it into the back of his belt. He'd had the key all along. He walked back to the cell, then undid the handcuffs from the bar and Runkles' wrist. As the deputy was rubbing his wrist, Pike took out Runkles' six-gun and shot him in the head. The gunfire was indeed loud in the confined space, but Pike was not worried that anyone would hear it. The thick adobe walls would deaden most of it, and there were few people out and about in town. Pike knelt and placed the weapon in Runkles' dead hand, then rose and headed for the door. After a careful peek to make sure no one was watching, he slipped out and around the building.

** ** ** ** **

"Evenin', Pony," Pike said from where he sat in a stuffed chair as the liveryman lit a lantern in his house. Stallings hesitated only a moment before he turned up the wick and looked at Pike.

"Strange to see you here," Stallings remarked, his voice uncertain.

"Reckon so, considerin' how well you played me

for a fool. I figure you'd expect me to finish up your dirty work for you and be long gone while you did whatever you were plannin' to do. Or maybe you were gonna find a way to put me in the boneyard to make sure I never came back to haunt you."

"You got a fanciful imagination, Brodie."

"I don't think so. Deputy Runkles and I had a nice chat not long ago."

In the lantern's light, Pike could see a worried look cross Stallings' face and quickly disappear. "Mind if I sit?" When Pike nodded, Stallings took a chair across the room from him. "Why should you talkin' to Runkles concern me?"

"He had some interestin' things to say about you, Pony."

"He's got a fanciful imagination too."

"He was too dim-witted to be fanciful."

Stallings nodded, having caught the meaning of "was." "So, what did he have to say?" He sounded more confident.

"Told me why you wanted Tilford and Bidwell dead and how you planned to get me hanged for the killing of Tilford. He didn't say how you planned to get rid of Bidwell, though."

"I had it figured out pretty well, with the lynch mob makin' sure you'd be hanged before a trial.

"Was Bidwell in the mob? He didn't seem the sort."

"Nope, but it didn't matter. I would've pressured him; blackmailed him, you might say, tellin' him I had proof that he had killed Tilford and the mob lynched you even though you were innocent. But it all got out of hand."

"So you had Gibbs—who Runkles said killed Tilford—and the others kill Yeager and North?"

"Oh, quite wrong, Brodie. I had hoped the mob would persuade Marshal Yeager to hand you over nice and neat. But the damn fool let you go."

"That wasn't a reason to kill him and Deputy North."

"No, it wasn't." For the first time, Stallings sounded angry. "Of course, we didn't know that at the time. Still, those idiots took it upon themselves to open fire and ended up killin' those two."

"Didn't upset you much, though, did it?" Anger had crept into Pike's voice.

"Not much, no," the liveryman agreed with a shrug. "But I wasn't happy about it either."

"That why you had me kill those men?"

Stallings grinned a little. "Yep. Seein' you all eager to get Yeager's killers gave me the idea all sudden-like."

"And you added Bidwell to the list to have me finish him off, too, so's your revenge against him and Tilford would be complete, eh?"

"Yep. Especially since my original plan had fizzled."

"There had to be more to it than them just gunnin' down the marshal and his deputy."

"Well, they were workin' for me and had been gettin' mighty uppity, and they'd been causin' trouble 'round town. I figured one day soon they were gonna get charged with more than petty crimes, and they might spill the beans about me havin' my hand in a number of businesses, some legal, others not, in town. I couldn't have that."

"No, I reckon you couldn't." Pike paused, then asked, "What were you plannin' to do about me?"

"Hadn't figured that out quite yet. I was mainly thinkin' you'd finish things up here and then light out, never to return since there'd be a noose hangin' over your head. I was also considerin' settin' a trap here for you and havin' Runkles back shoot you if that seemed necessary."

"Reckon I ruined all your plans." It was said with grim satisfaction.

"So, what are you gonna do about me?" Stallings asked.

"I think you know the answer to that, Pony."

"Yeah." Stallings' right hand inched down into the seat cushion. It stopped, and a shocked look came over the man's face when Pike said, "I found the pistol you had hidden there."

The liveryman gulped. He knew he had no chance, but he pushed out of the chair in a bid to reach Pike before the bounty hunter could fire. He hadn't gotten to his feet when a bullet from one of Pike's Colts stopped him in his tracks and knocked him back into the chair.

With disgust at having been duped rising in him again, Pike stood, spat on Stallings' body, and left the house. Ten minutes later, he was on his horse and riding out of Arrowhead.

CHAPTER 5

As he sat at his fire on the hill outside Arrowhead, Pike began to consider his future. He was a damn good bounty hunter and had brought in more than his share of hard-case outlaws to face justice. The events in Arrowhead had not been the first time he had been deceived or had tried to do good but had ended up somehow being on the wrong end. None of those times had sat well with him. And despite this situation ending with the criminals getting their comeuppance, and although no innocents had died at his hands, being made a fool of ate at him. Maybe it was time for him to give it up and find something else to do with his life.

He tossed out the dregs of his coffee and stretched out in his bedroll. He supposed he should have kept riding once he was out of town, but he figured no one would be coming after him, and if they did, they had no idea where to look for him. Still, aggravation with himself did not let sleep come easily.

In the morning, while he listlessly ate a meal of bacon and stale bread dipped in its grease, he wondered whether the townspeople would put out a handbill for his arrest. He decided it wouldn't happen. Few people in Arrowhead would even remember him, and fewer still would worry about the deaths of Woody Gibbs, Dunk Yost, Vin Jenks, and Ross Moss. He was certain Runkles had not made any friends since he had become marshal, and if the word got out about Pony Stallings' feud with Harry Tilford and Drew Bidwell, he would not be missed either. Pike figured he was safe from the recriminations of the people of Arrowhead.

After he finished his meager meal, he lethargically saddled his horse and loaded his sparse supplies, then rode northwest, deeper into the western mountains of New Mexico Territory and then into Colorado Territory. He had no plan on where to go, but he knew there were some nice, peaceful towns, some livelier boomtowns, and just plain good country in the southern part of Colorado Territory, which was bucking for statehood. What he would do there was a decision to be made as he traveled, but with every mile he rode, he was more uncertain about his future. With every mile, he grew more despondent about the way he had been duped—by a damn liveryman!—in Arrowhead.

Pike had been hoodwinked or made mistakes that came back to haunt him many times, but one of the worst was when it was something he didn't do.

** ** ** ** **

He had been on the trail of Jed Axelrod for a month back in '71, and he was getting frustrated about not being able to catch up to him. The outlaw was always a day or two ahead of him. Trail-weary and hungry for real food, Pike stopped in the town of Crooked Creek, Kansas. He perked up a little after a bath, a shave, and a haircut, as well as a new set of duds. A filling meal at a decent restaurant improved his mood a little more, and a stop at a high-class bordello made him feel very well. His frustrations were set aside for a spell as he sat in the Mud Puddle saloon, working on his second shot of rye and his first glass of beer.

This was, he thought, a good way to spend his time, and for the thousandth time in his latest quest for an outlaw, he considered finding another line of work. Then he smiled. Nope, he decided. He liked what he did and was good at it, despite some blunders along the way. He finished his drinks and headed to the hotel.

A peaceful night and a good breakfast had him considering staying in Crooked Creek for another day or two. He wasn't getting any closer to Axelrod anyway. Then he sighed, got his saddlebags, sniper rifle, and Winchester from his room, and headed to the livery stable. After he saddled his horse, he rode to the first mercantile store he saw and bought enough supplies to last him a few days, if he was watchful about how he used them. Then he was on the trail again.

A couple of days later, he broke his journey in the town of Pawnee Grove. His first stop was at the livery, the second at a hotel to get a room, and the third was at the marshal's office. The marshal wasn't there, but a deputy was.

"How can I help you?" he said.

"Lookin' for Jed Axelrod. You seen or heard of him in these parts?"

"Who are you, and why are you asking?"

Pike was a little taken aback by the harshness in the lawman's voice, then shrugged mentally, figuring the deputy didn't trust that he wasn't a fellow outlaw associated with Axelrod. "Brodie Pike. I've been hunting him for some weeks now. Keep just missing him."

"Bounty hunter?"

Pike nodded.

The lawman relaxed a little. "Deputy Ed Crane. You just missed him again. Rode in two days ago. Caused a ruckus in two saloons, threatened several people, and looked like he was gonna cause more trouble 'til Marshal Watts and I faced him down with a couple of shotguns."

"Why didn't you throw him the jail and hold him for a federal marshal to come get him and bring him back to Judge Collins' court?"

"Didn't know who he was at the time. Since he didn't really do much but stir up a little excitement, we brought him to the judge, who fined him twenty-five dollars, then we let him ride on out. A couple hours later, Marshal Watts found a circular on him, but we figured he was long gone by then."

"Reckon so."

"Apparently, he's one hard-case son of the devil."

"He is. You're lucky he didn't kill anyone in Pawnee Grove, includin' you and the marshal."

"After readin' the handbill, we know how lucky we were. We're good lawmen, me and Jim, but we ain't equipped for handlin' the likes of Jed Axelrod."

"Understood. Ain't many men who can stand up to Axelrod."

"You're one?" Crane asked, almost sarcastically.

"I hope to be, but I've been wrong before." He shrugged. "Well, reckon I'll spend the night here, then get back to trackin' him in the mornin'. Which way was he headed when you run him off?"

"South, mostly." Crane said, then, "Got a place to bed down?"

"Yep. Pawnee Arms."

"Good enough place. Decent restaurant is Peterson's over on Kiowa Street."

"Obliged." Half an hour later, Pike was finishing the last of his coffee and trying to decide whether a short stop at a saloon might be in order. He yawned and concluded it would not be wise if he wanted to get an early start.

Rested and with a full belly, Pike rode out of Pawnee Grove shortly after the sun came up. He headed south, but a mile outside town, he began roving east and west while still moving south, looking for signs of Axelrod's passing. He had been following the man long enough to know the outlaw's horse's hoofprints. Just before noon, he came across them. Judging by the tracks, Pike could tell that Axelrod was in no hurry. The bounty hunter picked up speed.

Hours later, he came upon an isolated sod farmhouse. A man stood outside in the fading sun, watching him. He stopped in front of him and said, "Howdy."

"Howdy."

"You seen a fella go by here recently? Five-ten or so, weighs maybe one-fifty. Gray shirt and hat, riding a mangy-lookin' chestnut."

The man nodded. "Was here a couple hours ago. Polite fella, he was. Broke bread with me and the family. Seemed a nice fella. Why are you lookin' for him?"

"That polite fella is wanted for a few bank robberies and at least two killin's. Been known to cause deviltry on farms out in the middle of nowhere."

"Don't believe that. None of it."

Pike shrugged. "Count your blessings that he didn't cause any harm to you and your family. Which way was he headed?"

"Southeast."

"Obliged." Pike touched the brim of his hat and rode on. He wished on the one hand that the man had invited him to stay the night. On the other, he was glad he had not. He crossed Bruckner Creek and spent the night in a grove of cottonwoods and willows. It wasn't a miserable camp since he had food, poor as it was, and coffee, but it wasn't the best either. He had hoped to have caught Axelrod by now, having been close behind him for the past day, but he had not. That had left him in a sour mood.

He pressed on the next day at a quick pace, and a few hours later, he spotted a town on the horizon.

He slowed and kept an eye on Axelrod's tracks, and he was surprised when they turned southwest, then northwest, bypassing the town. By now, Pike was certain Axelrod was heading for Indian Territory.

He hurried on. There was only one ferry across the Arkansas River in the area, and Axelrod would have to take that if he wanted to get to Indian Territory, where, Pike figured, Axelrod would feel safe.

Pike found the crusty old man who ran the ferry sitting in a well-made rocking chair outside his little shack, a corncob pipe clenched between yellowed teeth. The man didn't ask what Pike wanted; there was only one reason the newcomer was there.

"Fifty cent for you and fifty for the horse," the old man said in a raspy voice.

"Price is kind of dear."

The man grinned. "I can charge what I want lest you want to go to the next ferry twenty miles downriver. Ol' Custis there might charge you even more."

"I could just shoot you."

"Sure you could. Then you'd have to work the ferry across by yourself. Might be hard for a man not suited to such a thing, made all the more difficult tryin' to keep control of your horse while you're doin' it."

Pike grinned. "You got me there, friend." He dismounted and handed the man a silver dollar. "You had any other customers recently?"

"My customers are my business." He sounded defiant.

"If your last customer was who I think it was, he's

an outlaw headin' for Indian Territory."

"Five-ten or so, gray hat, flea-bitten horse?"

"That'd be him. His name's Jed Axelrod."

"Name doesn't mean anything to me, but I took him across about two hours ago. He didn't seem like he was in a hurry."

"Good. Now, how's about you get me to the other side so I can catch the son of a bitch."

"Get aboard. I suggest you walk the horse on and stay that way. Less chance of him getting' spooked and tossin' you in the water."

"Sounds like a right good idea. Let's go."

Soon enough, Pike was on the south side of the river and pressing onward. By midafternoon, he spotted a rider ahead. Considering the tracks he was following, he was sure the man was Axelrod. He hung back, not wanting to be seen, even though he didn't think Axelrod was watching his back trail. He stopped, loosened his cinch, and let his horse graze, then drank some water from his canteen, wishing there was a stream for the animal. He figured they would find something later in the day.

He waited for a half-hour or so before riding slowly on. A couple of hours later, he spotted a small fire in a copse along Crooked Creek. He rode up unhurriedly but veered several hundred yards to his right. He finally stopped, tied his horse to a bush after giving her some water, and followed the river through the trees.

In minutes, he was staring at Axelrod, who was sitting by a fire over which a frying pan was sizzling with bacon. It reminded Pike how hungry he was.

He stepped out from behind a tree, revolver in hand. "Keep your hands where I can see 'em, Mr. Axelrod."

The outlaw did so but asked, "Who the hell are you?"

"Name's Brodie Pike. Come to take you to Fort Smith or maybe Wichita since it's closer. Turn you over to the federal law."

"What in hell for?"

"Come, now, Mr. Axelrod, that's one mighty foolish question."

"Reckon it is."

"With your left hand, ease out your pistol and toss it yonder over the fire. Then lay on your stomach and put your hands behind your back."

Axelrod did so. Pike got the rope from its clasp on the outlaw's saddle, which was lying neatly on the ground under a cottonwood. He would put Axelrod in shackles later; he had not wanted to bring them with him as he crept through the trees lest the clanking give him away.

As Pike was starting to kneel to tie Axelrod's hands, he moved to holster his Colt. The outlaw surged up and rammed a shoulder into Pike's stomach, driving him back and down. The bounty hunter's pistol flew out of his hand.

Although he was having trouble breathing, Pike managed to get out of the way of the first fist thrown at his head, but he could not dodge the next. His head swam, but he was aware of Axelrod reaching for his other six-gun. Through the fog, he slammed a forearm into the outlaw's face, driving him back a little, but Pike dropped his Colt. That allowed

Axelrod to get somewhat groggily to his feet.

The outlaw charged again and crashed into Pike. The two fell, Axelrod partially on top of him. He shoved the outlaw off and got to his feet, wavering a little.

Axelrod jumped over the fire and swept his pistol off the ground, then turned to draw a bead on the bounty hunter.

Still fuzzy, Pike didn't think he had time to find either of his dropped Colts, so in desperation, he dove at Axelrod. The outlaw fired, and the bullet clipped Pike's ear. The bounty hunter's momentum drove him into the other man, knocking him down and sending his six-gun flying. Still dazed, Pike took two steps, picked up Axelrod's Remington, and thumbed back the hammer. He was about to pull the trigger when he stopped. Axelrod was basically helpless, and although he was an outlaw and killer, Pike thought even in his foggy mind that it would be wrong to gun him down.

"I ought to just put a bullet in your head right now," he said. "But I ain't that kind of fella. I am not disinclined to put a slug into one of your legs if you keep givin' me trouble, though. Now roll over on your belly and stay there quietly. One more move against me, and I'll plug you somewhere it'll hurt like hell but won't kill you."

Pike tied Axelrod's hands, then feet with the rope, which pulled the outlaw into a U and did not allow him to move much. If he shifted his legs, it tightened the rope on his hands; move his arms, and the rope on his legs tightened.

Pike went to the fire. Most of the bacon had burned, but a few pieces were edible, and he gobbled them down. The coffee was bitter, but it was still hot, and Pike enjoyed it. He went and got his horse, unsaddled and tended her, and brought her to the creek to drink again, then hobbled her so she could graze without wandering too far. Then he turned in, spreading his bedroll on the other side of the fire from Axelrod. He left the outlaw tied up as he bedded down.

"I can't sleep like this, dammit," Axelrod bellowed.

"I can add a gag if you'd like. If not, shut up and get what sleep you can."

Pike awoke in the morning sore but clear-headed. His ear had scabbed over. He found Axelrod's supply of bacon, cooked some, and reheated the coffee. As he ate, Axelrod said plaintively, "I'm hungry."

Pike got up and fed him a few pieces of bacon. "Ain't enough coffee for both of us," he said, "so you'll have to do without."

"You son of a bitch," Axelrod growled.

Pike just grinned at him. He "washed" the frying pan with some pebbled dirt, emptied the dregs of coffee from the pot onto the fire, and put them and the mug into Axelrod's saddlebags after he had tossed out the man's extra revolver and the cartridges he found there. Then he saddled both horses. He untied Axelrod and quickly shackled his hands before he could try anything. "Mount up," he said.

"I can't even stand," Axelrod snapped. "Bein' trussed up like that all night left my legs numb."

Pike grabbed him and hauled him up, then helped

him onto his horse, not a small feat. He tied the outlaw to his horse, and then they were off.

A few hours later, they arrived at the Arkansas. Pike fired his pistol into the air to attract the ferryman's attention, and not long after, the ferry arrived. "Two dollars," the man said.

Pike handed him two silver dollars and walked his horse and Axelrod's onto the craft. He left Axelrod on his horse.

Once on the north side of the Arkansas again, Pike followed the river until they reached Wichita. Pike had thought to follow the river to Fort Smith but decided toting Axelrod along was too much trouble to ride all those extra miles. He found a U.S. deputy marshal and handed the outlaw over to him. Two days later, he received the bounty for Axelrod and rode off, again following the river. This time he rode to Fort Smith, where he spent a few relaxing days at good restaurants, bordellos, and saloons. When he was rested, he picked up a handful of wanted posters, got a jail wagon and a mule to pull it, and crossed the river into Indian Territory.

Three months later, he was back in the city, handing off his prisoners and collecting the rewards. He learned that Axelrod had escaped on the trail to the court in Fort Smith only a few days after he had left Wichita. The escape was followed by numerous reports of stage and bank robberies—and murders.

"How'd he escape?" Pike asked one of Judge Collins' bailiffs.

"Federal marshal made it easy. Didn't exactly let him go but made sure shackles were loose and a revolver and a horse were handy. We learned about it when the marshal got here and told us. Sounded suspicious, so we talked to a couple of the other prisoners he had brought here in the wagon. They told us what had happened."

"Where's the son of a bitch now?"

"Who? The marshal or Axelrod?"

"Both, but for now, mostly the marshal."

"Down below in the cells."

"Can I see him?"

The bailiff cast a gimlet eye on him. "Don't think that'll be possible. Don't worry, though, Judge Collins will make sure he pays for it."

Pike nodded. "Any idea where Axelrod is now?"

"Last we heard, he killed a couple of Osage in the northern Indian Territory. It was said he also gunned down a farm family near Arkansas City up in Kansas. That's the last we heard of him."

"When?"

"Early last week."

Pike nodded. Over the next few hours, he gathered supplies, bought the mule he had used to pull the wagon, and filled up on a good meal. He was on the trail just after daybreak, holding the rope of the supply-laden mule. It was easy to follow Axelrod's trail from one bank robbery to the next and from the murder or assault of one farm family to the next.

As before, he was always a couple days behind and seemed not to be catching up. His frustration was building, and the long days on the trail with nothing to do but think about his failure haunted him. He should have killed Axelrod when he first caught him.

It was nothing new to him, to try to do something right or honorable and have it turn bad somehow.

It took more than two months, but he finally caught up to Axelrod on the open Kansas plains as the outlaw was trying to escape after robbing a bank.

When he spotted him, Pike dropped the mule's rope and kicked his horse into a gallop, and he closed the gap quickly. As if sensing someone was approaching, Axelrod looked at his back trail and saw Pike. He spurred his horse and raced off.

With a head start and a fresher horse, Axelrod began to pull away. "Damn," Pike growled, urging his horse to put on more speed. The animal responded, but Pike knew she could not keep up that pace, so he slammed to a stop, dismounted, pulled the Sharps from its scabbard, knelt, and brought the rifle up to his shoulder. With the horse racing away from him, and Axelrod bouncing in the saddle, Pike was not certain of the shot, but he fired anyway, ejected the spent shell, jammed home another round, and fired again.

Axelrod's horse went down, and the outlaw tumbled and rolled. Pike slid the Sharps into its scabbard, mounted his horse, galloped up to where Axelrod lay, and stopped sharply. He swung out of the saddle, drew one Colt, and walked toward where the dazed Axelrod was trying to pull a pistol. Pike fired, hitting Axelrod in the shoulder. He moved up to loom over Axelrod and kicked the outlaw in the chin, then booted Axelrod's pistol out of his hand.

"I should've killed you the last time I caught you,"

Pike said, his voice filled with anger. "Thought I'd do right and bring you in alive for the court to take care of you, but that scum of a bad lawman let you go, and you went on a rampage of deviltry. Not this time."

He fired the revolver again, and the bullet struck Axelrod in the stomach, then he put a bullet through Axelrod's thigh. As the man lay there writhing in pain, Pike said, "So long, you son of a bitch," and shot him in the head.

He mounted his horse, retrieved his mule, and rode off. He did not even bother to seek the reward on Axelrod's head. He had delivered justice, but only after his earlier decision not to kill this man had led to the deaths of a number of people. To him, it was a failure and a mistake.

CHAPTER 6

From where he sat on a bare hillside, Brodie Pike thought the place perfect. At the bottom of the hill lay an oblong grassy flat several miles long from left to right as best he could tell and a hundred yards or more across, sprinkled with trees. Heavy stands of cottonwoods, aspens, and spruces lined the far side of the meadow and crawled up the sides of a steep hill that stretched to the horizon in both directions. A two-foot-wide stream wove a snake-like course from his left across a small section of the clearing to disappear into the trees.

He rode down the slope and across the meadow. He found a glade in the trees would be just right for a small cabin. It was all he would need. He dismounted, unsaddled his horse, and made camp where his new home would be.

He had wandered a lot since he left Arrowhead in New Mexico Territory, thinking he should retire from bounty hunting. Although he was good at it, there had been mistakes, and he had been fooled too many times—by Pony Stallings and Asa Wilkins, among others—and made too many mistakes, as he had with Jed Axelrod. And the feud between the small ranchers and the Buckskin County Cattlemen's Association had led to too many deaths, for which he felt responsible. In his mind, those failures, as he saw them, overrode all the good he had done, so he figured it best to be off by himself for a while in a place where he could be free of people, good as well as bad, and hopefully be at peace. If he found an isolated place, he would make no more mistakes, and he would not be made a fool of. Here in southern Colorado Territory, he thought he had found that place.

In the morning, he wandered around the site, firming in his mind the placement and size of the cabin he would build. Eventually, he sat on a grassy stretch along the stream and let his mind wander. He was not sure this secluded spot was where he would stay, nor was he sure that solitude would be his life from now on. Doubts and questions plagued him. He had done nothing but live by the gun for more than a decade, so it was all he knew. He wondered what he would do with himself once the cabin was built. He decided he would deal with the future when it came. He laid back, pulled his hat over his eyes, and fell asleep.

** ** ** ** **

The dead men came alive, their arms with the skin flaking off and their faces peeling, reaching for him. "You killed me," they intoned. "I'm innocent. You killed me."

Pike reached for his revolvers, but his holsters were empty. His knife had disappeared, too. He turned to run, but his feet seemed to be stuck in mud, and he could move only at a snail's pace.

He turned his head. The men, or rather, the remnants of them, were closer and still coming, now moving faster. They continued to chant, "You killed me. You killed an innocent man! Shot me in the back. How many innocent people have you killed?" They held out clawed hands, reaching for Pike's neck.

** ** ** ** **

The bounty hunter woke with a start. drenched in sweat. He sat up and a shiver rippled up his spine, something that had never happened to him before. He swore at the memories that had brought the nightmare on him as he stood up shakily and took a few deep breaths to steady himself. Once he was back to normal, he headed to his campsite. The nightmare had spooked him, but it had also solidified his decision to keep himself distant from society. What he would do once his cabin was built and he had settled in was still a question, but he would deal with it when he reached that point.

He shot a large hare on the way, so he had meat for his supper. He skinned and cleaned it, then set it over the fire on a makeshift spit made of green branches. The nightmare was still vivid, and while he did not want to admit it, he was worried about sleeping that night. He put it off as long as he could before he finally closed his eyes. His dreams were unmolested by images of men he had killed, and he woke refreshed and with a better view on life.

Finished with his breakfast of leftover hare and coffee, he saddled up and trotted out of his site. Four days later, he rode into the mining town of Skeeter Creek. He had heard of the place when he'd stopped in the nearly empty town of Grass Gulch, two days' ride the other way in the San Juan Mountains. He had told a couple of men over a whiskey in the forlorn remaining saloon that he was looking for a booming mining town, and they'd mentioned Skeeter Creek. As he rode, he wondered what kind of place he would find. Many mining towns were abandoned as quickly as they rose, like Grass Gulch. To his surprise, Skeeter Creek seemed settled. There were a church, a school, a bank, twelve saloons, a bakery, a hardware store, a gunsmith, a butcher, two mercantile stores, and more, including a stamp mill north of the town. Another sign of the town's permanency was the number of prim and proper ladies strolling along the streets.

Being a mostly sensible man, he had put aside a decent sum from his bounty hunting, so he was not worried about getting what he needed even though prices in this mining town, like in most others, were high. Leaving his sniper rifle, Winchester, and saddlebags in the room he had rented, Pike spent a few days picking up living supplies, tools, nails, and other materials he thought he might need. He bought a small but serviceable farm wagon and a sturdy young mule to pull it.

Despite a renewed sense of uncertainty, he

decided to have a little spree before pulling out of town. He hadn't done so in quite a while, so he made arrangements to have the goods he'd bought stored in back of the mercantile. That done, he sat down to a good dinner, then wandered into a respectable-looking saloon and had two shots of redeye and a mug of cold beer. Finally, he went to a decent-looking bordello. It was not a top-of-the-line parlor house, but the building was well cared for, and it was a lively place.

The madam, a tall, almost-elegant woman of about fifty, greeted him, sizing him up as she did. She decided he would be able to afford the house's services.

"Evening," she said with a smile on her heavily painted face. "I'm Evangeline. Welcome to my house."

"Evenin'. Name's Brodie Pike," he responded. There was nothing more to say. There was only one reason he was here, and Evangeline, of course, knew it.

"Plannin' to stay awhile?"

Pike grinned. "Long as I can, I reckon. A man gets lonely, ridin' mountain trails."

"I would think so. Well, you're welcome to stay as long as you want. But ... well, you said you've been riding trails a while, and I must say it looks—and smells—like you've been doing so."

"A mite dirty, am I?" Pike considered taking offense but realized Evangeline was right.

"More than a mite, I'd say." There was no rancor in her voice, only humor.

"Well, I wouldn't want to offend any of the fine

ladies you have here. You have a way we can rectify this here unfortunate situation?"

"Sure. Cost you extra, though."

"Wouldn't think otherwise."

Evangeline grinned. "I'll have Ol' Pete, my servant, get a tub filled with hot water." She called out, and a tall, reedy black man poked his head through a doorway down the hall. "Start heating up a tub, Pete." She looked back at Pike. "That won't take long ..." Her voice trailed off.

"But?"

"Well, I don't think it'd be fitting for a fresh-cleaned man to put those foul-smelling clothes back on when he takes leave of my place. Not only would it be a shame for you, but it'd also be bad for business."

"I suppose you have a solution for that, too?"

"A choice. You can go over to one of the mercantiles—I'd suggest Whitten's—while Ol' Pete's getting the tub ready. Or I can have him go over there and get you a new outfit while you're busy upstairs." Seeing Pike's hesitation, she added, "Ol' Pete's good at sizing. He'll find duds that'll fit you well."

"Well, tell him to come see me, and I'll give him some money."

"Don't you fret about that. I have an understanding with Fred Whitten. He'll give Ol' Pete what's needed, and I'll add it to your bill here and pay Fred off later."

"Aimin' to take all my money are you, Miz Evangeline?"

The madam was ready to retort but then saw the small smile on Pike's face. "Of course," she said with a laugh. "I'm a businesswoman." She grew serious. "My prices aren't cheap, Mr. Pike, but they aren't avaricious either. You aren't special. I treat my customers—all my customers—well because I want repeat business. I won't charge you any more than the clothes costs, except for a dollar tip for Ol' Pete."

"Reckon you got a deal, Miz Evangeline."

"Very good," the madam said cheerfully. "Now, let's move into the sitting room, where your choice of my refined girls awaits your pleasure."

"No bath first?"

"Whoever you choose will be happy to help you with your ablutions. Now, come."

"Damn," Pike muttered a minute after he had entered the sitting room and surveyed the dozen women who had risen when he came in.

"What's wrong?" Evangeline asked, worried.

"Too damn hard to choose. Every one of these gals looks like she was made just for me."

"I can choose for you if you wish." When he hesitated, Evangeline said, "Etta, would you like to help Mr. Pike get cleaned up and then entertain him?"

"Oh, yes, ma'am," a slight blonde answered, head down, seemingly shy.

"No," Pike said. Evangeline looked at him in question. "I think she only said yes because you asked." He stared at the madam. "Be kind to her. She would've done what you asked, and I'm sure she would do well, but I'd prefer a gal who at least pretends to have some interest in me." Out of the corner of his eye, he caught one of the women moving half a step forward. He looked the others over more closely, then pointed at the one who had moved. "She seems like a fine gal."

"A good choice, Mr. Pike. Darcy, will you please accompany Mr. Pike to the bathing room? Ol' Pete should have heated water in there by now."

"Yes'm," Darcy said with a curtsey. She slipped an arm through one of his, ignoring the dust and the smell of sweat, and led him into a spacious room with three tubs, one of them filled with steaming water.

"I'll turn around until you disrobe and get in the tub. Would you like a shave?"

Pike scraped a hand across his stubbled jaw. "Wouldn't hurt." He shed his clothes and gingerly sank into the tub. "Ready."

Darcy came to the tub with a mug of shaving soap, a brush, and a straight razor. She wet the brush, whipped up the soap, and began lathering Pike's face.

"You're gonna ruin that pretty dress you're wearin'."

"It'll be fine."

"I doubt it. I bet you paid a pretty penny for it."

"What're you suggesting, Mr. Pike?" she asked in mock innocence.

"Shuck that nice dress and whatever else you're wearin' and join me."

"I'm not sure that'd be proper."

"You're bein' paid to do as I wish, ain't you?" he said with a wink. At her nod, he added, "Well?"

Within moments, she was nude and had climbed into the tub with him. She picked up the razor and went to work.

It was a night he would not soon—or ever—forget.

As he stepped out into the morning sunshine, he was thinking that perhaps he was being hasty in his plan to take himself out of society. The night's amusements and a new set of clothes had brightened his outlook on life, but a brief flicker of the week-old nightmare dashed the thought of returning to the life he had been leading. With a sigh, he headed for the livery stable.

He loaded up the wagon, covered the supplies with a large canvas tarp, tied his mare to the rear, and set off, his mind wrestling with his decision.

At his site, he carefully stored his supplies under canvas against the elements and laid out the lumber and the tools he would need. In the morning, he grabbed a saw, a hammer, and nails and went to work.

CHAPTER 7

Pike quickly learned that building a cabin by himself
was far from an easy task. He cut down a couple of
pines, then realized he had no way of stacking logs
to make a cabin. He decided that adobe would have
to do. And that meant another long trip to Skeeter
Creek to buy some lumber.

When he returned, he spent a day making frames
for adobe bricks. and then it was time to begin the
real work.

He was a strong, vigorous man, but spending a
week mixing clay, water, and straw and putting that
mixture into the three forms he had made, each with
thirty smaller rectangular openings, was exhausting
work. But he was not done. After the bricks had set
well, he removed them from the form and left them
in the sun to harden. Then it was time to fill the
forms again. And again. And again.

By the end of that week, he had made a few
hundred adobe bricks, and he needed a rest. He
took an afternoon to do some hunting and brought

down a small deer and two turkeys, then skinned and butchered them. He roasted part of a turkey and ate it with potatoes, savoring it all the more because he had convinced himself that he deserved it. As he was eating, he tried not to focus on the thought that he needed more than five times as many bricks as he had made.

After he was finished with his meal, he got two small airtight kegs from the wagon, both filled with salt. He took some of the mineral from each one and put it into another container. Then he took the hunks of deer meat and put them in one keg, covering them with plenty of salt. He did the same with the turkey in the other keg and placed the lids on tightly, then put both kegs back in the wagon and covered them with a tarp. He knew nothing about preserving meat this way, but it made sense to him, and he hoped it would work. He shrugged to himself. If it didn't, there was plenty of game about.

He went back to his fire and poured himself another cup of coffee. As he sat there sipping the thick liquid, he wondered again if he was doing the right thing. Making his way through life with a gun was all he knew. He had done well with it, but there were too many times, in looking back on his life, that despite wanting to do the right thing, he had made errors that occasionally led to trouble for him, or worse, for others.

On the other hand, he had no idea what he would do with himself if he wasn't out chasing outlaws and trying to bring some justice to the wildness in this untamed, belligerent land. As dusk slowly crawled over his camp, he looked across the meadow and found a small measure of peace. The future, he decided, would take care of itself. Or not.

In the morning, refreshed, he set about with his shovel and continued the slow, tedious work of making bricks. He fell into a rhythm, and the work went a little faster—not much, but some, especially after he decided to have the horse and the mule stomp through the raw materials rather than him working the mixture by hand. Still, he could work only so much more quickly at the chore. The sun would dry the bricks in its own good time.

After another week, he had more than doubled his supply of bricks, and for a break, he went to the logs he had chopped down his first day back from Skeeter Creek, cut them to the desired length, debarked them, and then used an adze to roughly square them off.

After another week of making bricks, he figured he had more than half of what he needed, so he decided it was time to start building the cabin. In the morning, he laid bricks for the back wall about twelve feet long and built it up to about four feet, then laid the southwest wall about the same length and height. Then it was on to the southeast wall. Sweating, he looked up at the sky. He still had at least an hour before sunset, but he decided he had done enough for the day. Besides, the supply of bricks had dwindled considerably.

The next day, he once again began the tedious process of creating more bricks. Until that was done, the three short walls would constitute his cabin.

"And a fine place it is," he said aloud with a chuckle.

Five days later, he had made another couple hundred bricks, and he was tired of the whole thing. Standing there looking across his valley, as he now thought of it, he decided another visit to Skeeter Creek and Evangeline's bordello was in order.

Mind made up, Pike shaved, then took a much-needed bath in the stream. In the morning, he hitched up the mule, tied his horse to the back of the wagon, and drove out.

Late in the afternoon four days later, he rode into Skeeter Creek and turned his wagon and animals over to the care of Butch Davies, the livery stable's owner.

Before he left the stable, Davies said to him, "Your mule needs new shoes."

"You can tell that when I just got here and you haven't even looked the animal over?"

Davies grinned widely. "Tell by the way it's movin'. I knew this mule before I sold it to you. I can see the change right off."

"I think you're just tryin' to drum up business for the farrier," Pike said, but he chuckled.

"Could be. He is my cousin," the liveryman said with a laugh. "But it's true. This critter needs new shoes."

"See to it, then." Pike left and headed straight to Evangeline's.

"Well, lookee here," the painted madam said with a smile. "If it ain't Mr. Brodie Pike. Been a while."

"It has. Been busy."

"You look a little more presentable than last time,

but still ..."

"I know. I gussied myself up before I headed here, but that was four days ago. Reckon I could use some more cleanin' up."

"As you know, we can arrange that. I'll have Ol' Pete start fillin' the tub." She turned and shouted for the servant and gave him instructions. Then she said, with a touch of sadness and worry, "I'm afraid Darcy is occupied."

"I reckon you have a few others who might take her place," Pike said with a grin. "Like last time, though, I'd prefer a gal who's willin'."

"They're all willin', Mr. Pike," Evangeline said with a hearty laugh. "It's why they're here! But I know what you mean. I think I got just the gal for you. Come." When they had entered the parlor, she beckoned to a tall, slender, red-haired beauty. "This is Fiona."

"Howdy, Fiona."

"Welcome," she responded.

"I think you'd be a good partner for Mr. Pike. What do you think?"

Fiona boldly appraised him. "He'll do," she said and released a delightful laugh.

"Then I'll leave you two to your pleasures."

** ** ** ** **

Refreshed and more than a little tired, Pike headed to Cable's Hardware and bought a small flat-top iron stove, though he didn't know how he was going to get it off the wagon and into the house. He also replenished his supply of lumber, nails, and other building materials he thought he might need, then it was off to Whitten's Mercantile to restock his foodstuffs.

Last he went to Davies' livery. He checked to make sure the mule had indeed been newly and properly shod. It seemed to annoy Davies, but Pike didn't care. Finally, he paid the liveryman and had him and his assistant hitch up the wagon, and with his horse tied to the rear, he drove back to Cable's. He untied the horse so Cable's two hired men could load the stove onto the wagon.

Finally, Pike tied his horse to the rear of the wagon again and headed out of town. It did not take him long to realize he was being followed. When he came to the first fork in the road a few miles outside Skeeter Creek, he took the left branch instead of the right. He didn't know where it went, but he hoped it would lead back to his valley, even it was longer. He soon found a place where he could pull off the trail and be partially hidden. He hoped he was being overly cautious and that no one was really following him, but it became evident that there was still someone on his trail.

He drove the wagon behind some rocks, untied his horse, mounted it, and waited. Before long, three men slowly rode up. They appeared to be town men who wanted to seem tough. They were about Pike's age, and while they were armed, they didn't have a killer's eyes or mien. Pike rode into the middle of the trail in front of them. "Howdy, boys."

The three stopped, and one nervously said, "Howdy."

"I can't help but wonder why you boys've been followin' me."

"That's preposterous," the same man sputtered. "We're headed to Mayville."

"That so?"

"Sure is," the man said, trying to sound indignant.

"Then you boys are lost." He pointed northeast. "Mayville's that way, I believe."

"We're takin' a shortcut."

"Like hell you are," Pike snapped. "There ain't any shortcut here if the place you're supposed to be goin' is in a different direction. Now, I don't take to people followin' me. When they do, they usually mean trouble. I'm not fixin' to ride where I'm goin' with you fellas on my trail the whole way."

"But we ..."

"You're bein' a pain in my rump is what you are. You mind tellin' me why you're so interested in me?"

"We're not ..."

"I'm gonna tell you this just one time: Go back to Skeeter Creek and don't ever bother me again."

"Or?" one of the other men asked, trying but failing to sound as if he were a hard case.

"You really want to challenge me, boy?" Pike asked in a voice that was truly hard.

"Maybe I am." His voice quavered.

"You have a death wish? Go back home, boy, and let me be. You got no call to be followin' me, and if I catch you at it again, I'll kill you—all of you—and anyone else foolish enough to come against me."

"You have no right to talk to us that way," the first one said, showing a little anger as he tried to hide his newfound fear.

"That's enough, Alf," the third man, who had been silent until now, said in a commanding voice. "We apologize for our inadvertent encounter. We'll not bother you again."

"That'd be wise. For your sake."

The third man nodded. "Let's go, Alf, Cullen." He turned his horse and rode off. The other two waited only a moment before, with angry glances at Pike, they followed.

Pike sat on his horse for a quarter of an hour, wanting to make sure the men hadn't doubled back. Then he hooked the mare up to the back of the wagon again and got on his way. He decided to continue on this road to see where it would take him. As dusk was closing in, he was beginning to wonder just where this road went. He found another place where he could pull off the trail and get a modicum of seclusion. It was dark by the time he finished caring for the animals, so he settled for a small fire, a couple of pieces of cold chicken, and some coffee.

As he traveled the next day, he wondered why the men had been following him. The only reason he could think of was that they wanted to know where he was staying and perhaps why he was in the area. It couldn't be, he reasoned, that they wanted to rob him. Still, he wasn't sure, and he would have to be vigilant.

By midday, he found that this road led to the main road he used to get to Skeeter Creek. It was not a shortcut, just a loop. Pike had no trouble as he arrived back at his homesite and took up his work again. It was slow and tedious, but he was used to it and labored steadily.

The adobe bricks piled up, and in another couple of weeks, he figured he had enough to finish his rudimentary house. First, though, he had to get the stove inside. He tied a rope around it and dallied the other end to his saddle horn. Moving the horse slowly forward, the rope tugged on the stove until it fell to the ground. He pulled the rope up closer before dallying it again, then rode the horse, dragging the stove, through what would be the front of the house. Once it was near where he wanted it to be, he unhooked it, hobbled the mare, and let her out to graze, then "walked" the stove into a corner of the room.

Then the stacking of the adobe bricks began again. While he worked, he had the sensation that he was being watched.

CHAPTER 8

Pike heard horses and looked up from where he was laying another brick on the northeast wall. Half a dozen warriors—Utes, he figured—were making their way slowly across the meadow. He set the brick into place and unhurriedly grabbed his gun belt from where it hung on a corner of the wagon, which he had pulled close to the house so he could lay bricks up high. He gave a moment's thought to moving inside the partially finished dwelling until he saw what the Indians wanted, but they did not appear to be rushing to attack. Besides, they might figure he was lying in wait for them. He buckled on the twin Colts, walked out a few feet, and stood waiting, arms across his chest.

The six Utes stopped a few yards away and a young, strong-looking warrior dismounted and strode forward, arrogance dripping from his dark countenance. He was about twenty-five, Pike figured, and of medium height with a strong physique. He wore a plain calico shirt, a buckskin breechclout, leggings, and moccasins. A bow and a quiver of arrows were slung across his back, and he had a sheathed knife and a tomahawk stuck in the cord that held up the breechclout.

The Ute stopped with his nose almost touching Pike and began yelling in his own language. He continued for a minute or two, then slowly circled him, still hollering. The warrior finally stopped when he came around to stand in front of Pike again, this time a foot or so away. He looked over his right shoulder, smirking as his companions grinned.

As the young Ute was turning back to face the white man, Pike smacked him across the face with his full strength. The blow snapped the warrior's head around and made him stumble. Angrily, the warrior jerked around, only to stagger back another step and almost sink to his knees as Pike slapped him even harder with his right hand.

The warrior steadied himself and took a step toward Pike. Blinded by his rage, he did not see Pike's hand resting on the grip on one of his Colts. At least one of the others did, though, and he barked two sharp words at the young man, who, seething, fought to bring himself under control.

Pike scanned the other warriors but saw no immediate danger. Keeping a wary eye on the hotheaded young man, he addressed himself to the one who had spoken. "You the leader of these fellas?" When the Indian nodded, Pike asked, "You speak English?" Another nod. "My name's Brodie Pike. You?"

"Blind Bull."

"Who's this fractious young man?"

Blind Bull smiled. "He is Crazy Hawk."

Pike stared at him for a moment before deciding the war leader was not joshing him. "I was gonna chide you for not teachin' him any manners, but with a name like that, maybe he can't be taught any."

"Maybe true. He asked what you're doin' here, white-eye."

"Took him a damn long time to ask such a simple question."

"He also said some things about your ancestors and your manliness before and after."

"Like what?"

"He seems to think your mother was, how do you say it, very close to a demon. He also called you a skunk-humper." Blind Bull was trying to stifle a chuckle.

"Well, my dear ma was a saint, you understand. Wouldn't ever have anything to do with demons, so that ain't true. As for me bein' a skunk-humper, well, that can't be true neither. If it was, Crazy Hawk'd be my son."

There were a few moments of silence, then Blind Bull roared with laughter, followed a heartbeat later by all the other Utes except Crazy Hawk.

When the laughter dwindled, Blind Bull said, "You must answer. What are you doin' here?"

Pike did not like the hardening of the warrior's attitude and was not about to be bullied. "Buildin' a house."

"Why?"

"So I can live in it."

"Why?"

"Need a place to live." He managed to hide the smile of satisfaction at Blind Bull's growing frustration and annoyance.

"This is our land, white man," Blind Bull snapped.

"I don't see any sign that says so," Pike snapped back. When he saw the Ute's annoyance rise, he relented. "Ah, hell, Blind Bull, don't mind me. I'm just bein' contrary 'cause I don't like bein' prodded." He paused, looking past the warriors at the mostly bare hillside behind them. "I'm just lookin' for a place to settle down away from people."

"Trouble in the east?"

"You could say that, though it's mostly in the south," Pike said with a shrug.

"So, what will you do here?"

"Don't know. Ain't thought that far ahead yet. Might start a small ranch, I suppose, raise some cattle or horses."

"Bring many people, start a town, maybe?"

"Ain't damn likely. Like I said, I come out here to get away from people. I ever get tired of bein' alone, I'll go back to where there are people, not bring people out here where there ain't any."

Blind Bull looked at Pike, his gaze unwavering, as was that of the object of his observation. It was quiet except for the usual sounds here—the sighing of the wind through the trees, horses clomping hooves now and then or neighing softly.

Finally, the Ute leader nodded. "You may stay. For now."

"Gee, I'm obliged for your kindness," Pike said,

unsure of whether the sarcasm made an impression on Blind Bull.

The war chief said something to Crazy Hawk in his own language, and the still-seething young warrior mounted his pony. Blind Bull started to turn his horse to leave but stopped at Pike's voice.

"One more thing, Blind Bull. I ain't aimin' to cause any trouble, so I'd be obliged if you were to make sure Crazy Hawk keeps his wits about him. That young man has a mighty hot streak in him, and I wouldn't think it beyond him to sneak back here of a night and try to put me under. He does, the Utes'll have one less warrior to help protect them from their enemies."

Once more, Blind Bull stared at Pike as if judging his character. Then he nodded. The Utes swung around and galloped off.

Pike took a deep breath and let it out slowly. That had been tense but seemed to have worked out well, except for the wild card that was Crazy Hawk.

** ** ** ** **

Pike was certain that Crazy Hawk would be back but would probably wait a night or two. It took three, but Pike had remained wary. He kept his fire in the same spot each night, but he changed where he set his bedroll. He woke a bit before dawn with an urge to visit the bushes when he sensed more than heard someone. He lay there breathing slowly and evenly, though he moved his head to the left. Moments later, in the light grayness of almost-dawn, he spotted a slight movement. He smiled, then eased out a pistol and rolled onto this side. The sound of him cocking the Colt was loud in the quiet, and the movement stopped.

"I'm over here, Crazy Hawk, not where I was last night. Now stand up where I can see you."

There was no sound or movement for almost a minute, but the gray had lightened just enough for Pike to pick out the shadowy lump he figured was the Ute. He fired just to the right of it, and the bullet whined off a rock.

"Next one won't miss, Crazy Hawk." More silence. "Ain't no reason for any killin' here today, boy. Let's just go and set by the fire and break bread together. Talk this out."

Still nothing. Pike sighed in annoyance. Crazy Hawk had not had a gun the other day, and Pike guessed he did not have one now. He also figured the young Ute had planned to kill him up close with his knife or tomahawk. He rose, and with uncocked pistol in hand, walked toward the lump. When he got within a few feet, Crazy Hawk jumped up and charged.

Pike half-turned and lowered his shoulder. The Ute, unable to stop, slammed into the shoulder full on his chest. He dropped to the ground, losing his knife and struggling to breathe.

"Damn fool," Pike muttered as he slid his six-gun back into the holster. He held out his hand, but Crazy Hawk slapped it away.

"I'm about out of patience with you, boy," the bounty hunter said. He grabbed Crazy Hawk's calico shirt and hauled him up, then shoved him toward the fire. "Sit," he ordered. When the Ute did not do so, Pike kicked his feet out from under him, and the man fell. He started to get up, but Pike shoved him back down, grabbing the Ute's tomahawk as he did. Still having a little trouble breathing, Crazy Hawk shifted so he was sitting.

Pike tossed the Ute's tomahawk toward the house, then poured coffee from the small pot into the only cup that was handy and set it in front of Crazy Hawk. He sat on the other side of the fire.

"Bein' shamed in front of others is a hard thing for a proud man to accept," Pike said softly. "Sometimes pride is all a man has, and there's times when a man has to respond with strength to insults. But sometimes a proud man can use such a thing as a lesson. If he has any sense."

Crazy Hawk said nothing, just continued to glower at Pike. He did, however, take a sip of coffee, wincing at its bitterness.

"Instead of tryin' to kill me, you should learn something from what happened the other day."

"I learned a good lesson. I learned not to trust white men. I learned it's better to kill a white man right away. No trouble later."

"Well, those're lessons, I reckon. Not very good ones, though, I'd have to say."

"No? What should I have learned, eh? To just walk away after bein' insulted just because you're a white man?"

"Not really, but it'd be better than getting yourself shot dead."

"Not if I killed you first."

"You seem to think that'd be easy, and that is a damn-fool way of thinkin' about a situation like this." He paused. "No, Crazy Hawk, the lesson you should have learned is to know your enemy before makin' an ass of yourself."

Crazy Hawk jerked as if he had been slapped again.

"You didn't see me, Crazy Hawk. All you saw was a white man, and you figured you'd come snappin' and snarlin' right in my face and I'd piss my trousers." He could tell by the small reaction in the Ute's eyes that he had come close to the mark. "Such thinkin' without thinkin'," Pike added with a small grin, "is a good way to get put under. Ain't every white-eyed demon afraid of a strutting pissant Ute."

Crazy Hawk scowled.

"Wasn't but a second after you dropped off your pony that I knew you were nothin' but a swaggerin' little fart who thought he was a lot tougher'n he really is. It's why I didn't see any call to do anything. Had I figured you were really tough and not just a posturin' snot, you'd have been a dead man before you started circlin' me."

"So would you be dead. Blind Bull and the others would've filled you full of arrows."

"Likely I would be. But I can guarantee you, Crazy Hawk, that there'd be at least one more of your people, maybe even a couple more, gone under as well. Even with those two fellas over to my right sittin' there with nocked arrows, I could still get off a few shots."

Crazy Hawk looked even more sour, his face

contorted with anger and frustration.

"And all that—two, three, maybe four good men dead because you wanted to strut around like a peacock, thinkin' you were gonna scare hell out of me but not knowin' a damn thing about me. Foolish, boy. Damn foolish."

While Crazy Hawk continued to seethe, Pike rose and pulled some meat from a bag hanging from a nearby tree. Back at the fire, he held out a chunk. When the Ute did not reach for it, Pike snapped, "Oh, for chrissakes, boy, take it. Maybe you can work off some of that anger by chewing."

Sullenly, the Indian took it. Pike sat back down and gnawed on the hunk of roasted elk.

CHAPTER 9

Crazy Hawk tried to kill Pike again the next night. And the night after that. And the night after that. By then, Pike had had his fill of moving his bedroll each night and having to sleep with one eye open. On the fourth night, Pike did not even make a pretense of sleeping. He simply waited in the shadows, leaning against a corner of the house, estimating where the Ute would steal into the camp.

Crazy Hawk was stealthier than usual, but Pike became aware of him quickly. When the Indian was three feet away, still unaware of the statue that was his quarry, Pike said quietly, "Over here, boy."

The Ute turned in time to have Pike clout him a good shot in the forehead with his pistol barrel. The man staggered and wobbled but did not fall.

Pike holstered his revolver, slipped a shoulder under one of the Ute's arms, and helped him to where the fire was just embers. He dumped Crazy Hawk and stoked the fire, then poured two mugs of coffee, set one in front of Crazy Hawk, and took a seat on the log with his own tin mug in hand. He sipped a little, watching the Indian, who seemed to be regaining his focus.

"Drink up, boy. It'll help you recover some."

Crazy Hawk did not hesitate as he had the first night, but he looked no happier as he drank.

"This is the second time I could've easily killed you but didn't. Come to think on it, I could've done so last night and the one before instead of letting you run off when you learned I wasn't gonna be tricked. I didn't do it then, either."

"You're afraid."

"Of what? You? That don't make any sense." Pike chuckled.

"Of my people. You kill me, and they'll come for you. Kill you. Take your hair. Maybe something else, too." He tried to grin but couldn't quite accomplish it.

"Reckon they could, but I'm thinkin' that wouldn't happen. Blind Bull and the others seem to have a heap more sense than you do. They'll know that killin' me won't be easy. They'll also figure that if some of the white officials in this territory hear that the Utes've killed a white man, they'll face hard times."

"Then why do you not kill me? You afraid of killin'?"

"I've killed far more men than you have," Pike said with a harsh note in his voice. "A lot more. And many of 'em were tougher'n you are. I didn't kill you because I didn't see any need to, and I didn't want to cause trouble here. Like I told you and Blind Bull and the others the other day, I aim to settle here, and I don't want any trouble. I just want to be left in peace, and that includes getting a restful night's sleep without worrying about some hotheaded young buck tryin' to kill me."

"I'll keep tryin'."

"No. You won't," Pike said flatly.

"Why not?" Crazy Hawk asked, surprised.

"Because the next time you come after me, I will kill you."

Crazy Hawk stared at him, and in the flickering orangish-red light of the fire, he could see that Pike was utterly serious and confident in his simple statement. Still, the Ute had little fear. "Maybe I'm hard to kill, too, eh?"

"Maybe, Hawk, maybe. But it doesn't have to come to that. I won't get any joy out of killin' you." He grinned just a little. "Or bein' killed by you. Maybe you'll feel like a big man if you manage to kill me, but that doesn't accomplish anything."

"It keeps you from makin' light of me again."

"Ah, yes, a young man's pride. It's a good way to get yourself killed before you can watch your family grow."

"Are you so weak you have no pride?"

"You know, Hawk, every time you open your mouth, something more foolish comes out." Pike sighed. He was tired of this but agitated, too. "Like I said, I just want to live here in peace. I don't want to be feudin' with you. No reason I can see why we can't get along."

"Every time I see you, I'm filled with anger."

"Then don't come 'round here. Stay in your village

and leave me be."

"Blind Bull and the others laughed at me. I can't face them or any of my people because of that."

"Sure, you can. If you're as tough a fella as you think you are, you can. Hell, go on back to the village and tell everyone me'n you had a good talk and you spared my life 'cause I'm only a foolish white-eye."

Crazy Hawk drank a little coffee and thought that over.

"No man who has any pride at all likes being made a fool of, especially in front of people he cares about. He ..."

"That ever happened to you?" the Ute demanded.

Pike sighed again. "More than once."

"What you do about it?"

"Sat and sulked for a spell, then moved on. 'Course, I didn't have to live with those people all the time like you do with Blind Bull and all. But it drove me away from those people, too."

"You didn't kill them?"

"Some, but they gave me no choice. It was them or me."

Crazy Hawk sat in silence for a bit, then said, "You have given me much to think about, white-eye. I'll do that." He started to rise but grimaced as pain rocked through his head, and he plopped back down. "Damn, how am I supposed to explain this?" he muttered, anger replacing the contemplative spirit from the moment before.

Pike gave a small laugh, bordering on a snort. "Anybody asks, tell 'em you were out waterin' the flowers and tripped over a rock or tree root and banged your head. You wouldn't be the first fella who's done so."

"You are a sneaky man, white-eye."

"My name's Brodie Pike, not white-eye, redskin." He had a moment's pleasure when he saw Crazy Hawk stiffen. "And while you're thinkin' on all this, don't come skulkin' around here. Like I said, you do, and I'll kill you."

"You'll try. But I won't. If I decide I must kill you, I'll come at you like a warrior. Face to face."

"Can I trust you?"

Pike could see the anger rise on Crazy Hawk's face, then fade. "Yes," he said simply. He managed to get to his feet this time.

Before he could leave, Pike said, "I was wonderin' one thing. Why'd it take Blind Bull, you, and the others so long to come and see what I was doin'? I'd been here several weeks by then. I don't expect your people'd let me get my house halfway done before comin' over to see what I was doin' here."

"We were far east, huntin'. Otherwise, we would've paid you a visit before you even got started."

"Figured. How was the huntin'?"

Crazy Hawk shook his head. "Buffalo're gettin' mighty scarce, but we made out good enough. Next year could be bad, though." He clamped his mouth shut. This was not the time or place to speak of such things. He spun and headed into the trees.

A minute later, Pike heard a horse trot away. He sat for a little longer, sipping the last of his coffee and pondering what would happen with Crazy Hawk. He wondered if this would be another time when he tried to do right but it turned out badly. He tossed the dregs of his coffee into the fire, carried his bedroll into his almost completed house, and went to sleep.

As he worked the next morning, Pike wondered what he should do about the situation. All his talk about swallowing humiliation was, he thought, hogwash. A prideful man—and Crazy Hawk was certainly that—could not just walk away from humiliation. No, some recourse was needed. The trick was, Pike thought, was in how to let the Ute regain his pride without letting himself be killed.

He put it out of his mind as he loaded a bunch of bricks into the wagon, then had the mule draw it up close to one side of the house. After unhooking the mule and turning it out to graze, Pike climbed into the wagon and began setting bricks in place.

He spent the next two days doing the same things and then decided the structure was as tall as it needed to be. He hacked down two dozen straight though not thick trees and cut them to length, then hewed notches in carefully measured spots on the logs. That done, he called it quits for the day.

The next day he managed, with the help of the mule, sufficient rope, and a whole lot of strength and sweat, to get the logs atop the walls, fitting the notches into each other. He retrieved two large tarps, laid them over the logs, and tied them to pegs in the outside wall of the house. They would be his roof for the time being.

As he sat down to a meal of turkey and cornbread, he thought about the interior of the house. He might, he realized, have to make most, if not all, of the furniture he would want. He could buy it in Skeeter Creek, but that might attract unwanted attention. With those townsmen already having followed him, he did not need more trouble or people knowing where he was. Problem was, he had never made any furniture and was sure he could not manage it. Finally, he decided with a sigh of resignation, seeing as how he had no idea of how to make anything except maybe a simple plank table, he would have to make a trip and buy some, hoping not to have to shoot someone trying to find out what he was doing, and where and why.

It was while he was contemplating his carpentry skills, or rather his deficiencies, that the seed of an idea was planted for a way to make amends with Crazy Hawk. He was surprised he had not seen the Ute lately, and he wondered if there was trouble on the horizon.

The next day he made more adobe bricks, and by midafternoon, he had quite a few baking in the sun. He roamed the forest for a while to see if looking at the various trees would give him any idea about what if any furniture he could make and how to do so. It soon became apparent that his idea of buying the items would be the only way to furnish his house.

As he was loading the bricks on the wagon in preparation for putting on a more solid roof, he saw Crazy Hawk riding up. He quickly wiped his hands on an old shirt and buckled on his gun belt, then moved away from the house a little to greet the Ute.

"Howdy, Crazy Hawk," he said, stopping.

The warrior halted about five yards from Pike

and slid off his pony. "Howdy."

"You come here peaceable?"

"I came to make you pay for humiliatin' me."

"You think killin' me will erase that shame?"

"Yep. Blind Bull and all the others in my village will know that I am a proud warrior who'll take no insult from anyone, especially a white-eye."

"And how will they know that?"

"I'll show 'em your scalp."

"I was afraid you were gonna say something like that, but that won't be so easy to do. I could just shoot you down here and now and be done with it."

"You're afraid to fight me."

"Nope, but I won't if I don't have to. I think I got a way that will keep us from havin' to do battle with each other."

"How?" Crazy Hawk sounded skeptical. "I think you're afraid."

Pike explained his idea.

Crazy Hawk looked at Pike as if he had gone loco, then said, "If you lie, we will kill you."

"I ain't lyin'."

CHAPTER 10

Crazy Hawk, Blind Bull, and the four other warriors who had first approached Pike rode up in midafternoon, but they were not alone. Five other warriors and two women had also come along.

Pike did not like the extra people. He pointed. "They weren't part of the arrangement, Crazy Hawk," he said. "You broke your word."

"You are afraid?" Crazy Hawk challenged as he dismounted. Much of the Ute's original cockiness had returned.

"No, you walkin' pile of skunk scat. I'm damned angry. The deal was you'd show up with the men who were here that first day, not a bunch of others and a couple women besides."

"You breakin' the deal?"

"Nope. You are." Pike looked at Blind Bull, who was still mounted, as were the others. "You always allow your people to break their word? I thought you people said the white men were the ones who always did that."

"I didn't make deal with you. You and Crazy Hawk made deal. He told us this was all right. That all were welcome."

"Well, then he lied to you."

Blind Bull shrugged. "That's between you and him. You want to back out, we go. You and Crazy Hawk face each other alone or not fight."

Pike stood there and thought about it, his anger growing. He didn't mind so much that other warriors had come along, but the two women were another story, especially since one was young and lovely. He finally sighed. "Get on with it, Crazy Hawk, but only what we agreed on. You do more, and there'll be hell to pay for you."

As Crazy Hawk strutted forward, Pike said, "And don't get too cocky, boy, or I'll shoot you down regardless of what your friends might do."

That took a little wind out of the Ute's sails, but not much. He swaggered as he approached Pike.

"You take another step like a struttin' peacock, and I'll humiliate you worse than I did the last time."

Crazy Hawk started to retort until he saw the look in Pike's eyes. He continued walking toward Pike without the arrogance.

The bounty hunter braced himself as Crazy Hawk stopped in front of him. Crazy Hawk hauled off and slapped Pike's right cheek as hard as he could, snapping his head to the side. He did it again to the other cheek.

Pike shook his head to clear it. It had stung a lot more than he had thought it would, but he would recover quickly. He nodded at Crazy Hawk and asked, "Satisfied, boy?"

The warrior stared at him for a moment, then let loose a loud, ululating war cry, pumping his fist in the air.

A chorus of whoops rose from the other Utes, including the women. Crazy Hawk spun and ran to his horse. Leaping on, he whirled the animal around several times before taking off at a gallop, yipping loudly as he went. The other Utes followed at a trot.

Pike covered his jaw with a hand and wriggled it as he watched the Indians ride off. He thought he saw the young woman glance back ever so briefly at him with a smile, then she was gone. "Nah," he finally muttered. "She didn't do any such thing. Just as well. She wouldn't respect me anyway." With a sigh of relief, he turned and headed back to his house, though he quickly realized he was in no mood to do any work just now.

But he was back at it the next morning, and over the next several days, he finished the roof, hammered in the door and window frames, and mixed up more adobe to coat the outside of the house and fill in the gaps. Since he didn't want the mixture to dry and harden too quickly, he made small batches and spread them on, letting it dry after it was applied.

He was just finishing the third wall when Crazy Hawk showed up and dismounted. He seemed friendly. "What the hell're you doin' here, Hawk?"

"Visitin' friend."

"You got no friends here, boy." Pike was more than a little irritated. He was tired of dealing with the Ute, and despite the drudgery, he wanted to get back to his work.

"You and me, we're friends now."

"You're sure livin' up to your name, Crazy Hawk, especially the crazy part."

"I think you maybe need a friend. You're all alone."

"That's the idea, boy. Bein' alone is why I'm here. I figured on bein' away from folks."

"You just don't like me 'cause I'm an Indian, as you white-eyes call us."

"That ain't true, but you can think that if it'll get rid of you."

"You're on Ute land. You need friends."

"I regret not havin' killed you the first time I saw you."

"You're gonna make me cry."

"Bah. Go away, dammit."

"Go wash that dirt off you. I'll make sure coffee's on. Food, too, if you got any."

"Barrel under the wagon has some deer meat," Pike said, resigned to the fact that Crazy Hawk was not going to leave him alone anytime soon. He headed to the stream to wash up. When he got back to the fire, the Ute had put coffee on, and there were two thick hunks of meat dangling over the flames, their fat dripping and sizzling.

"I didn't figure you even knew how to put a coffeepot on the fire, let alone cook up meat."

Crazy Hawk grinned. "Who do you think makes food when we go on the warpath?"

"Reckon you do. Never thought about it before."

They drank coffee in silence, then started gnawing on the deer meat. Between bites, Pike asked, "So, what're you really doin' here, Hawk?"

"Come to learn about you."

Pike gave put a short laugh. "What'n hell for? Ain't much to learn anyway."

"You're an interestin' man. I can learn much from you."

"About me? Or about white men?"

Crazy Hawk grinned. "Maybe both. But now you tell me what you do before you come here."

"Bounty huntin'."

"What is that?"

"Huntin' bad men to bring 'em to justice and getting paid for it."

Crazy Hawk looked surprised. "White-eye leaders pay you to hunt these men?"

"Yep. The money is called a bounty. That's why it's called bounty huntin'."

"And you say I'm loco?" He shook his head in amazement.

"How'd you come by the name Crazy Hawk anyway?"

"My people don't mean crazy the way yours do. To us, it means spirited, maybe you say. Like a war pony eager to go."

"And Hawk?"

Crazy Hawk grinned again. "Hawks are fierce and protective, mostly. Of course, they're noisy and troublesome, too." He laughed.

"Fits you well."

The Ute grew serious. "I must know about the white man. My people must know about the white man. They are closin' in on us more and more every year. I'll fight. Others, too. But the time will come when fightin' will end. I'll die before then, but if I learn about white men, I can teach others."

"Not much I can tell you that'll help."

"Why do you say that?"

Pike shrugged. "In some ways, I ain't like most white men.

"Why?"

"Reckon I ain't as greedy as some nor as land-hungry as others."

"But you're here takin' our land."

"Am I? I just want a little piece to live on. I ain't plannin' on tryin' to drive you off it or even layin' claim to it. I'm just borrowin' it from your people."

"You won't farm?"

"Do I look like a damn farmer to you?"

Crazy Hawk grinned. "Reckon not. Maybe you'll be a rancher. Take our land to raise cattle, create trouble, bring in men to help, make more trouble."

"You become a shaman all of a sudden and can tell what'll happen in the future?"

"No. It's just the way white men act. They see land they want and take it."

"The government signs a treaty with you and pays you for the land."

"Your government signs papers with a chief who doesn't have the right to give away our land."

"If the chief signs it, then it should be in effect."

"Reckon it's time I gave you a lesson in the ways of the Utes and other tribes. There are major bands of our people as there are with most other tribes. Within those bands are smaller bands. Most villages have only a few families. My village has seven, no, eight families. That's large, but not too big. All tribes I know of don't have an overall chief. Each small band has its own civil chief, but he doesn't have any more say than any other warriors."

"A chief has no power?" Pike asked, surprised.

"Nope. Not like your government does in the one called the Great Father. One of my people becomes a chief because of his brave deeds as a young man and his wisdom as an older man."

"So he can't make decisions for your people?"

"Nope. All the warriors get their say, then a council of elders makes a decision. But that's only for the tribe's village. A chief's words might be given more significance, but he can't tell 'em what to do."

"I never heard that before. To me, that don't make sense. Folks need someone in charge to make decisions for the people. We do something called voting when we elect our leader. Or leaders. It'd be like you choosing a chief for each of your major bands and choosing a chief over all the bands."

"That's damn foolish."

"Not to me," Pike said with a chuckle at the absurdity. "Your way sounds damn foolish to me."

"Our way is better,' Crazy Hawk insisted.

"Reckon you and I ain't gonna be able to agree on this."

"Reckon not," the Ute said with a nod.

"Maybe now that you know how the white men do these things, your people'll stop breakin' whatever treaties you do sign, even if they don't cover all of you."

Crazy Hawk stiffened in anger. "If your people understood how we do these things, we might not have to break 'em. Besides, your government breaks treaties more often than we do."

Pike sighed. "I don't know that for sure, but I reckon there's more truth to it than not."

They were silent for a while before Pike said, "I reckon we both learned something today."

"Yep. Maybe you ain't like most other white-eyes, as you say, but you taught me something about the white men's thinkin'."

"I don't think it'll do you any good, but maybe it'll help your people sometime when you deal with whites comin' to take your land." He paused, then asked, "Where's that leave us?"

"What d'you mean?"

"I don't want to have to worry about you comin' to take my hair every time some other white man makes you angry."

Crazy Hawk laughed. "The only time I'll come for your scalp is if you make me angry."

"Don't take much."

"Reckon not. But it's strange for me to say we're friends now. Yes?"

"Reckon so."

CHAPTER 11

Crazy Hawk rode up, followed by a woman who towed a horse pulling a travois. Pike heard him and came out of the still-barren house, where he had been setting the stovepipe in place. He recognized the woman as the one who had been with Blind Bull and the others when Crazy Hawk counted coup on Pike. He grew a little uneasy, thinking she might not consider him manly.

"Howdy, Crazy Hawk," he said, wiping his hands on an old piece of cloth.

"Howdy." Crazy Hawk slipped a leg over the saddle horn and slid down the side of the horse.

"What're you doing here?"

"Brought you some things."

"And who's this delightful lady accompanyin' you?" Pike appraised her, but she kept her head down.

"She is my sister," Crazy Hawk said dismissively. "Little Raven."

"You don't sound like you think much of her, Hawk. Why's that?"

"She's just a woman."

"Then why'd you bring her?"

"Needed someone to hold horse with travois." Then he grinned. "She also said she wants to meet the crazy white man building a house of dirt."

"It ain't dirt. It's adobe," Pike said with a laugh. He turned toward Little Raven, who was dismounting. He liked what he saw. She was short, considerably shorter than his five-foot-eleven, and seemed shapely, though it was hard to tell for sure with the heavy decorated buckskin dress she wore. Her face was round and dark, with high, prominent cheekbones and almost black eyes. Her hair was long, jet-black, parted in the center, and hung in two braids. "Nice to meet you, ma'am," he said.

He wasn't sure if she was ignoring him or too shy to respond. He looked back at her brother. "What'd you bring?"

"Something for sittin' and something for sleepin'." He nodded at Little Raven, who began unfastening the ties on the travois.

Pike was tempted to help her but decided that would not be appreciated by either Ute. He watched as she tugged off a buffalo robe and carried it into the house. She repeated the trip twice more, then took a wooden contraption that Pike could not figure out and deposited that in the house too. A second one followed.

"I can guess what the hides are for, Hawk, but what'n hell're the two other things?"

"For resting your back against. They're made of willow mostly. Little Raven is setting them up. The buffalo robes are for sleepin', of course."

"Obliged. But why?"

"You got nothin' in your lodge. You need soft place to sleep and somewhere to sit so you're not all bent over from sittin' on a log."

"You're too kind," Pike said with a dose of sarcasm in his voice. He figured Crazy Hawk did not get that.

Little Raven came out of the house and smiled shyly at Pike. "Go inside," she said. "Try."

Pike went inside, followed by Crazy Hawk. The latter sat easily and leaned against the willow backrest. Pike gingerly did the same, not certain the flimsy-looking thing would hold his weight. He was pleasantly surprised when it did and by its comfort. "Nice," he said. Spotting Little Raven standing just outside the doorway, he said, "Come on in, Little Raven."

"She's good outside," Crazy Hawk said.

"Maybe your people treat women like that, but mine don't, or at least I don't. Or maybe it's just you. But if I ask her to come in, she should come in. You got nothing to say about it."

"I say no."

"You're puttin' our new friendship to the test already, Hawk, and I won't have it. I'll let it pass this time, but if you do it again, or if you mistreat her, I'll take strong exception to it. You don't want that, do you?"

The Ute stared at the white man for some moments, then said, "No. Friends should not fight, eh? But you got strange ways."

"I could say the same about your people."

Little Raven stood in the doorway, uncertain. Pike nodded at her. "It's all right, woman."

She entered and sat with both legs to the right on the dirt floor between Pike and her brother but a little closer to the former. Pike noticed but said nothing about it.

"Wish I had some food or even coffee to give you folks," Pike said, sounding apologetic. "But I wasn't expectin' company." It bothered him, not because it might seem unthoughtful but because even coffee would keep Little Raven here longer. And that, he suddenly realized, was important. But it was not to be.

"The robes good?" Little Raven asked.

"I expect they will be. Better than sleepin' on the hard ground in an old bedroll, which I been doin' for way too long."

"Is good." Her English was halting and accented but understandable.

"I won't be able to use 'em right away, though." When both Utes looked at him in surprise, Pike added, "I need to go to town to get supplies and such. I'll be gone for more than a week."

"You be back?" Little Raven asked.

Pike thought she was worried. "Yes, ma'am. Soon's I can. Skeeter Creek has its attractions, but I don't fancy spendin' much time there."

"You wait. I'll take Little Raven to village, then come back here and go with you."

"Ain't necessary, and it could be dangerous for you. I don't expect the folks in Skeeter Creek'd take kindly to a Ute showing up in town."

"They put up with a few old Utes going there, but not a warrior like me. I'll stay away, but I'll show you a different way to go."

"A shortcut?"

Crazy Hawk took a few moments to catch on to the meaning of that, then he shook his head. "No. Different way. Few people know. Even most of my people don't know. Might help you someday."

"Reckon it might." He told Crazy Hawk about being followed that time when he went to town and how he had to confront those men and take a roundabout way back to his house. "It big enough for a wagon?"

"Yep. But hard to find and narrow in many places. Some caves to spend the night."

"Reckon I can wait a day or two while you take Little Raven home and return. Plenty of work for me to do yet."

"What'll you do when you finish all your work?"

"What makes you think I'll ever get finished?" Pike countered with a laugh.

A few minutes later, he watched as the two Utes rode northeast. He was surprised by the melancholy that struck him. He didn't think he'd miss Crazy Hawk much. Then he realized with a shock that it was the sight of Little Raven disappearing that saddened him. "I'll be damned," he muttered. Then he shook his head. A visit to Evangeline's might be in order, he thought.

** ** ** ** **

"How far's this cutoff, Hawk?" Pike asked as he tied his horse to the back of his wagon moments after hitching the mule to it. It was three days since Crazy Hawk and Little Raven had left. The warrior had arrived yesterday afternoon bearing a freshly butchered hunk of deer meat.

"About a day's ride. Little more, maybe."

"Then lead on," Pike said as he climbed aboard the wagon and clicked the mule into moving.

An hour later, they came to the road that ran to Skeeter Creek, which lay northwest of Pike's house. Several hours after that, they stopped for the night in a glade. Pike tended to the horses and the mule while Crazy Hawk gathered wood and built a small fire. Coffee was soon made, and meat from the deer they had not eaten the previous night was cooking.

In the morning, at the Ute's suggestion, Pike gathered what grass and willow shoots and bark he could and put it all in the wagon bed. Crazy Hawk gathered firewood and piled that in the wagon as well. "We'll need it. "Little wood where we go."

Pike nodded. Then he hitched up the mule, and they rode on.

In the late afternoon, Crazy Hawk stopped Pike and pointed at a massive boulder and a patch of ash, hackberry, and juniper trees.

"You're joshin' me, Hawk."

"Nope. Looks like there's no place to go, but come around this side of rock and look just the right way. There's space to get between rock and trees."

Pike looked skeptical, but he did as he was directed and found to his surprise that with a close look, there was an opening. It could be seen only by someone who was actually looking for it, and even then, it took a change in perspective.

"Go on," Crazy Hawk urged.

Pike shrugged, and after some maneuvering, he got the wagon past the boulder with little trouble. The road beyond rose steeply before flattening out. Pike was surprised that the road was passable, with great stands of pines on the sloping northeast side and a sharp cliff tilted toward the road on the other. The angle kept the trees from growing into the road.

"Old buffalo trail," Crazy Hawk explained as he squeezed past the wagon to take the lead. "And path for my grandfather's people to take when heading to war with the Navajos."

Pike shrugged and followed the Ute up the trail. While it was open, it narrowed considerably in places, requiring all of Pike's attention lest the wheels of the conveyance run off the side. It was not a comfortable ride, but Pike supposed it could have been worse.

It began to get dark in the shadow of the cliff, and Pike worried about driving the wagon on the narrow trail in the dark. Crazy Hawk soon stopped next to a cave dug into the cliff wall. "We stay here."

"Sounds good to me," Pike said as he gingerly climbed off the wagon.

Again they shared duties, with Pike tending the animals and making sure they had some of the forage he had gathered and stored in the wagon. Crazy Hawk started a fire with the fuel they had brought along.

The next day, as Pike hitched up the mule, Crazy Hawk took much of the remaining forage and firewood and left it in the cave for their return journey. They went along with pretty much the same slow, careful travel. There were many hours of nothing for Pike to do but make sure he kept the wagon from toppling down the slope. It was exhausting and nerve-wracking, and he was glad when they called it a day at another cave, one of several they had passed. This one was very large, big enough to bring the animals in and still have enough room for the men to spend the night.

Pike did not look forward to the next day's travel, but it had to be done. He was thankful it was less stressful, with the trail widening.

Just before noon, Crazy hawk stopped. "Way back onto the road is here." He pointed.

Pike looked at him. "I'll take your word for it since you were right about the other end, but it sure doesn't seem to be a way onto the road."

"It's there. I'll go ahead and make sure the way is clear, then I'll come back. I stay here while you in town, wait for you."

"All right. I won't be back 'til late tomorrow or maybe the day after."

"I'll wait. I got enough food. Think you can find this way again?"

"Don't know 'til I try. Unless there's trouble, I might just take the regular road back. Be a lot faster that way."

"Also maybe more dangerous. You make choice."

CHAPTER 12

Pike wasn't certain, but he thought he was being followed again, and he was a little worried about finding the entrance to the cutoff as he plodded along. His nervousness grew with each yard he traveled. There was not much difference in the trees or the mountain that rose to his right. As with the other end, the entrance on this side would not be easy to spot, even though he had tried to note it when he pulled out of it yesterday.

Then Crazy Hawk appeared in the middle of the road. He nodded at Pike and led the way in a serpentine route through trees and brush. Then he was on the mountain road again.

"Looks like you got a full wagon there, Brodie," Crazy Hawk said as they sat down to a supper of beef and biscuits and coffee Pike had brought from town.

"It is. Table, couple of chairs, a door, oiled paper for the windows, couple barrels of lime."

"What is lime?"

"A soft rock or something. Mix it with water and

use it to coat the adobe on the house. Protects it some from the weather."

Crazy Hawk laughed. "You white-eyes got no sense. Seems a heap of trouble. Live in a tipi like we do. Warm in winter, cool in summer."

"So's adobe."

"Maybe, but a skin lodge is easy to put up and take down, and it don't have to be cared for like adobe. And it's comfortable in rain or snow or anything else."

"You might have a point. I'll have to try a tipi one day, see if I like it."

"I reckon you will."

"Well, if you were to invite me to the village, maybe I could see how they are."

"Thought you'd be scared of visitin' my people."

"I might be," Pike said with a chuckle, "if I figured all the people are as fractious as you are."

Crazy Hawk grinned, proud of the description. "What else did you get?"

"Nails, a new ax, various food, salt," Pike told him with a shrug. "Nothing to interest you, I reckon."

"Whiskey?"

Pike looked at the Ute in surprise. "Didn't think you'd let yourself be tempted by such a thing."

"Whiskey's bad most times. Good sometimes."

"Well, you ain't gettin' any from me. All's I need is a testy bastard like you runnin' 'round full of tanglefoot."

"Bah." But he grinned, then grew serious. "You followed?"

"Ain't sure. Thought I might be, but I never saw

anyone."

"Want me to take a look?"

"Nope. Not unless you figure they know this route."

"Not even most of my people know this way."

"Then no need to get your ass shot up on my account."

Crazy Hawk wasn't sure how to take that, so he just stuffed another piece of beef in his mouth.

** ** ** ** **

When Pike awoke at the campsite half a day's ride from his house, Crazy Hawk was gone. As he stoked the fire to heat up the coffee in the pot, he growled, "Son of a bitch doesn't want to help me unload the wagon." Then he grinned. "Well, can't say as I blame him."

He ate a leisurely breakfast, then headed slowly toward home. It was afternoon when he arrived at the house, and he was relieved to see it was still standing and no one or nothing had damaged it in the more than a week he had been gone. He unhitched the wagon and tended to the mule—the horse needed little care—and turned it and the mare out to graze.

After a brief meal, he set about unloading the wagon. He wrestled the furniture into the house, along with the food and related supplies. At last, he nailed the door on leather hinges to the jamb. After another barely sufficient meal, he stretched out on the buffalo robes and fell asleep with no problem.

The next day, with considerable reluctance, he

began preparing the lime mixture and eventually started coating the walls of the house. It was tedious work, though less so than laying the adobe bricks. It was still monotonous, so he was glad to see Crazy Hawk, who rode up and dismounted with a genial, "Máchaa."

"Figured you'd show up after the work's all done."

"Warriors don't work on the lodge." He grinned.

"Far's I can see, warriors don't do much work at all." Pike wiped his hands on a rag. "What're you doin' here this time?" He tried not to sound disappointed that Crazy Hawk had arrived without his sister.

"Huntin' is work." He laughed. "Fun, but work."

"So, why're you here instead of out huntin'?"

"Came to find out if you wanted to see how real people live."

"Eh?"

"Invite you to the village."

"I'll be welcome?"

"Likely." He grinned. "Might be a few who don't like white-eyes, but others'll be all right with it. A few might even welcome you, like Blind Bull."

"And you?"

"We're friends."

"So?"

"I will ... not scalp you." He burst into laughter.

"Good to know, Hawk," Pike said flatly.

Still laughing, Crazy hawk said, "There's one maybe will be happy to see you."

"Who's that?" Pike asked, a hint of hope in the words.

"You'll find out when we get there. Maybe."

Hope not quite dashed, Pike asked, "How long will it take to get there?"

"We leave now, we'll be there tomorrow before the sun is high. We wait 'til morning, we'll arrive late, likely just before dark."

"Well, if it won't bother you none, I'd as soon wait 'til the morrow. I got a little work to finish up, and I'll need to get cleaned up."

"Is good."

"You're welcome to sleep in the house."

"Nope. I'll sleep out here. Bein' in a dirt house is no good for a man."

"Suit yourself." He went back to work.

** ** ** ** **

Pike wasn't afraid when he and Crazy Hawk rode into the Ute village just before dark the next day, but if forced, he would admit to being nervous. He had never seen a place like this: buffalo-hide tipis scattered around seemingly haphazardly, smoke hazily drifting from the tops, racks of meat drying, and large dogs roaming about. Buckskin-clad men, women, and children were engaged in various activities, though they stopped to stare at Pike for a minute or two before returning to what they had been doing.

Pike searched for Little Raven, and he finally spotted her standing outside one of the lodges. He thought she smiled at him.

Crazy Hawk stopped them outside a tipi where Blind Bull and an ancient warrior stood. "Many Snows," Crazy Hawk said to Pike. "Our village chief.

Much respected."

"Honored to meet you," Pike said awkwardly, not sure how to respond.

Many Snows looked up at Pike with a stony stare, then grinned a toothless but open grin. "You welcome," he said.

Pike relaxed a little.

"Come," the chief said. "We smoke, talk." He turned and stepped into the tipi. Blind Bull followed him.

Pike and Crazy Hawk dismounted, gave their horses to a couple of boys, and went inside, where they sat around a small fire.

Pike watched what Many Snows did with the pipe, which was lighted by Crazy Hawk, and tried to emulate the actions. He figured he did well enough when no one complained.

After the pipe had made a full circle, Many Snows put it aside and said, "I no speak English good. Understand good. Crazy Hawk will speak my words to you."

Pike nodded.

Many Snows spoke briefly with Crazy Hawk in their language, then the latter said to Pike, "The chief wants to know what your plans are here."

"I told *you* that."

"Yep. He wants to hear it from you."

Pike shrugged again. "Don't know what my plans are beyond livin' a life of quiet for a spell."

"You no bring others?" Many Snows asked.

"Nope."

Many Snows spoke more in Ute, and Crazy

Hawk translated, "White men're tryin' to take more of our land. Talk of new treaty, which'll be bad for my people."

"I got nothin' to do with that. I got no dealin's with the government, soldiers, or anybody else lookin' to take your land. I ain't a farmer lookin' for land, nor a miner lookin' for gold or silver. Like I told Crazy Hawk, I might run a few cattle for myself, but no more. I don't ask anything of you and your people other than to leave me in peace on that small hunk of land. I don't aim to bring others here, nor fight your people."

"Why do you do this?" Crazy Hawk asked for Many Snows.

"I'm tired of huntin' down men and maybe killin' 'em for money. Too damn much killin'. I've had enough of it."

"You're afraid?"

"Nope. Just want to get away from it."

After listening to Many Snows again, Crazy Hawk said, "He wants to know if you can be trusted."

"What d'you think?"

Crazy Hawk was silent for a few moments, and Pike began to wonder. Then the Ute turned to the chief and nodded. "I trust him," he said.

Many Snows looked at Blind Bull, who also nodded. "Is good," the chief said. "Now we eat."

Many Snows' two ancient wives passed around bowls of stew with small chunks of meat floating in it and tin mugs of coffee.

"This ain't dog meat, is it?" Pike asked Crazy Hawk in a whisper.

"Dog is good. Tasty." He and the others laughed. "No. It's elk. Fresh, too."

Still dubious, Pike dug in and found out that it was, indeed, elk, and it was very good. As he ate, he found himself a little surprised to hear the Utes talking as he would with friends, if he had any. Making small talk, smiling, arguing a little, laughing. He had always thought Indians were reserved most times, even though he had come to know Crazy Hawk as a joker.

The sound of drums began outside, and Many Snows said, "It is time."

"Time for what?" Pike asked.

"Dance. In your honor," Crazy Hawk explained.

"I ain't expected to dance, am I?"

"Nope, but you can if you want."

"Doubt it," Pike said as he rose and followed the others outside.

CHAPTER 13

Pike sat on a log watching the dancers, Little Raven, Blind Bull, and Crazy Hawk among them. The old chief, Many Snows, sat nearby, leaning against a willow backrest. He seemed to be dozing. The bouncing stutter-steps of the Utes were interesting but held no draw for Pike. Even though the drums invaded his blood, he had no desire to join the dancers. He could not even do normal white folks' dances, let alone try these seemingly aimless steps.

After a little while, he looked around the village, seeing a little more than he had when he arrived: racks with warriors' weapons, children playing or trying to emulate their eiders in dancing, and a sense of joyfulness. Yet he thought he could also detect weariness around the place, a feeling of forlornness. Not quite despair but a sense that the Utes had seen better days and the future was not all that bright for them. It saddened him. While he didn't know these people well, he had come to be friends with Crazy Hawk, and he certainly liked Little Raven, but to see the inhabitants of the village becoming a less-than-buoyant people in the not-so-distant future was disturbing.

He shook the feeling off as he looked back at the dancers. All appeared to be enjoying the activity, giving themselves over to the joy of the movements, the pulsating throb of the drums, and the singing. It was all strange to Pike, but the Utes were swept up in it. He wasn't sure if there were words or just sounds. Either way, the Utes gave full voice to it. Maybe, he thought, he was seeing shabbiness that wasn't really there.

Blind Bull broke off dancing and approached Pike. "Come, join us," he invited.

"Reckon not," Pike replied with an apologetic grin.

"Little Raven wants you to."

"No, I can't do it. I'm too clumsy. If I danced anywhere near her, I'd end up mashing her toes with these big ol' boots of mine."

"Told you he was not a real man like us," said Crazy Hawk, who had wandered over.

"Just you go on back to pretendin' you know what you're doin' out there," Pike said. "It looks to me like you're full of firewater and just stumblin' around, tryin' to keep from fallin' on your face."

Crazy Hawk and Blind Bull laughed and danced back through the circle of women to join the men.

As the pulsating drums reverberated through him, Pike reconsidered his choice not to join the Utes. Before he could finalize his decision, Little Raven danced over to him and held out her hand.

He shook his head. "I can't do it."

Little Raven pouted, then smiled. She grabbed his hand and pulled him reluctantly to his feet. He was about to argue and try to break free and flee, but she headed away from the dancing. Wondering what was going on, he allowed her to tow him along.

She stopped at the entrance to a tipi and pulled back the flap, waving a hand at the opening. Still uncertain about all this, he entered. She followed. He turned, and she moved up and threw her arms around him.

Surprised, he gingerly placed his arms around her. He hadn't realized until now how small she was compared to him. She couldn't be much more than five feet tall, he figured, and while she wasn't slim, she was nowhere near chubby either.

"Take off clothes," she said, pulling back from him just a bit.

"What?" he asked dumbly, not sure he had heard right.

"Take off clothes. Me too. We have good time together, me and you."

"You sure?"

"Yes." She began unbuckling his gun belt.

"This is Blind Bull's lodge, isn't it?"

"Yes."

"What if he comes back?"

"He ask if you enjoy self, then maybe do same with one of his wives."

She got his gun belt off and tossed it aside, and Pike winced at the mistreatment when it landed with a thud. Little Raven began working on the buttons of his shirt.

"Wait," he said, grabbing her wrists gently. "This don't seem right somehow."

"You afraid?" She looked up at him questioningly. "You not like women?"

"No, I ain't afraid. And yes, I like women very much."

"You not like me, then?"

"I like you quite a bit, but most women I know ain't so free with their favors."

"Then white-eyes women are fools. They miss much fun. This is okay here. We like. Do all the time."

"With anybody?"

"If we like."

"So if we were to ... uh, join here now, tomorrow you could be doin' this with someone else?"

"Yes. If like." She smiled up at him. "I like you most."

He freed her wrists and rested his hands on her hips. She went back to unbuttoning his shirt. He lifted a hand, and with his index finger under her chin, raised her face. He wasn't sure if this was proper or even known by Ute women, but he bent to kiss her. If it was unknown to her, she accepted it and learned quickly.

In minutes, their clothes were lying in small, messy piles, and the two were entwined on the buffalo robes. Pike began exploring Little Raven's lush body, enjoying it more every second. Then they were coupled and rising to waves of pleasure that soon exploded, sending shocks of elation through them both.

"Is good?" Little Raven asked when her breathing

had calmed a little.

"No," he said with a grin she could not see because both were lying on their backs. When she tensed, he added, "Better than good. Much better. Wonderful."

He rolled onto an elbow and saw the smile on her lips. It pleased him, and he flopped back down.

Before long, she rolled onto her side, her breasts against the side of his chest. Her hand reached for him. "Again?" she asked playfully. "You're ready, I think."

"I believe I am."

They were slower and more deliberate, taking their time and unhurriedly building the passion in each other until it was time to join again.

Just as they were doing so, Blind Bull and his two wives entered the lodge. Pike froze. The Ute looked at his daughter and the white man and grinned. "Is good?" he asked with a chuckle.

"Yep," Pike managed in a strangled voice.

Little Raven dug her fingernails into his back, urging him to get on with the pleasurable business at hand. Pike gave in to the urging, immediately forgetting about the warrior.

** ** ** ** **

Pike awoke foggily, the night's pleasures having sapped him. Little Raven was dressed and squatting by the fire. She heard him shift and push himself up so he was sitting.

"*Tick-û-arr-a-way?* Hungry?" she asked.

"Yes." Embarrassed, he rose and began pulling on his clothes, grateful that Blind Bull and his wives were gone. When he was dressed and had plopped down next to her, she handed him a bowl of elk stew and set a mug of coffee beside him.

"Thanks."

"You feel good?" Little Raven asked.

"Sure do." He grinned at her, then shoved a spoonful of stew into his mouth.

They were silent while Pike ate, then Little Raven asked, "Why you not sayin' anything?"

"I ain't sure what to say." He was angry at himself. He had not been so tongue-tied with a woman in years, not since he had found himself in the clutches of a soiled dove when he was sixteen and ... He pushed that thought out of his mind but still was uncertain and annoyed by it.

"You talked much yesterday."

"That was different. Somehow."

"You not like me now?"

"Hell, yes, I like you. But you're different in some ways."

"Different how? I'm not a woman?" She was starting to show some irritability.

"Oh, you're a woman, all right. But I've never been with a Ute woman before, and I ain't sure how to act."

"Act like with any woman. Utes no different from white women."

Pike thought about that for some seconds, then shook his head. "Well, no, but yes." Seeing her confusion, he went on, "Like I said yesterday, white women ain't as forward as you. Most don't seem to like ... to want to do ... what we did last night."

"White women are fools."

"Reckon they are," Pike admitted. "But they're taught that such things ain't proper and that givin' themselves over to such doings is sinful. Bad in the eyes of God—the Great Spirit, you might say."

"But they have many children." Little Raven seemed perplexed.

"Yep. But they do it because they're supposed to. Because God wants 'em to have children. Lots of 'em. But they ain't supposed to enjoy it."

"They're ur-nip-in-gen—crazy!" She sounded incredulous.

"Reckon you're right. I think a lot of white men like it that way. Maybe it's 'cause they don't have to worry much about their women doin' such things with other men. Keeps 'em under their thumb. Or something." He shrugged. He couldn't explain it any better, in large part because he didn't understand it himself.

"White-eyes are strange."

Pike laughed. "I can't argue with that."

"You're not like that."

"Mostly, no. 'Least, I hope not. 'Course, if I have a woman, I don't want her beddin' another man." He glanced at Little Raven out of the corner of his eye, wanting to see that she understood he was making a point and what she might think about that.

"If a man takes care of his woman, she won't do that. She stay with her man."

"Even when he's away for a spell?"

"Yes. If he likes her most and she likes him most, they be together."

Pike set down the bowl and reached for her. Little Raven came easily and eagerly into his arms. "I like you most," he whispered.

"I like you most, too," she responded, and she raised her face to be kissed.

Shortly they were once again naked and tumbling into the robes, heedless of time of day or if anyone would enter the lodge. Their focus was on each other. Ultimately, they came to shuddering climaxes and fell apart, gasping for breath.

At last, Pike rose and dressed. He went outside to take care of business. When he returned, Little Raven was also dressed, looking demure but pleased. She handed Pike a mug of coffee.

"You go soon?" she asked, sorrow in her voice.

Pike nodded. "Got to get back to my place and make sure nothing's happened while I been away." He smiled softly. "You'll miss me?"

"Yes."

"Good. I'll be back in a few days."

She nodded sadly.

"It's true. I aim to see you again soon's I can."

Little Raven smiled, her spirits lifting.

"You'll not do ... this with any other man while I'm gone?" he asked nervously.

"No. I for you."

Pike smiled, relieved.

CHAPTER 14

Pike opened his door and stepped halfway out of the adobe house, then realized he had forgotten something. He turned to head back inside when an arrow thudded into the door where his chest would have been had he not turned. Another arrow immediately followed. Pike pushed back inside and slammed the door shut.

He peered through the crack between the jamb and the door, but he could not see where the ambush had come from. He didn't know if there was one Indian out there or a whole war party. It was early afternoon, and he realized it was going to be a long day. He could not risk trying to go outside again without knowing his attacker or attackers had fled.

He supposed he could slip out through one of the windows, but there was too much open space between the cabin and the edge of the tree line to make that a viable alternative.

So he paced around the small house, occasionally looking through the cracks around the doors and windows to make sure whoever was out there was not planning a frontal assault. At one point, he eased the door open, reached around, and plucked one arrow free. Sometime later, he did the same with the other arrow. Neither action provoked another assault, but he thought that might be because his arm was not an enticing target.

It was a long, boring, and aggravating afternoon. He hated being cooped up, but he had no liking for the idea of being killed by an arrow fired by an unknown assailant. Face to face, he'd take on just about anybody, but being killed by a specter was not something he was about to accept. Several times he considered making a break for it, figuring whoever was out there couldn't be very comfortable either and might not want to spend his whole day waiting to kill Pike whenever the bounty hunter stepped out of the house, but he decided it was too risky. He spent some of the time cleaning and oiling his Colts, keeping one loaded and near at hand as he worked on the other.

As dusk neared, however, he decided it was time. He opened the door just wide enough for him to squeeze out. Crouching, he darted toward the trees to his right. Once in the forest, he straightened up and took his bearings. He had an idea of where the arrows had come from and headed toward that place in a roundabout way, moving as quietly as he could. He winced every time a branch snapped under his foot. He eventually neared the suspected spot, and soon after found where someone had been lying behind a rock. He nodded, glad he had found signs but annoyed that he had spent the entire afternoon confined to his cabin.

He didn't think the Indian would be back that night, but the possibility, however small, made for a restless night's sleep.

Before dawn, he was up and made himself a quick meal of bacon and leftover cornbread. It was still dark when he slipped outside and saddled his horse. Although he was still concerned that an enemy was lurking, he rode off. By the time daylight was on him, he was a few miles down the trail.

He knew he was being watched later that afternoon as he neared the Ute village, but he did not falter. As he rode past the first tipis, he spotted Crazy Hawk coming out of his lodge. He rode straight to him and stopped in front of his friend. "Howdy."

"Howdy. You're back soon."

Pike dismounted. "Yep. Got something to discuss with you."

"Sounds serious."

"It is."

Little Raven, who had moved quietly up next to him, took the reins of Pike's horse. "I take care of her. You talk to Crazy Hawk."

"A moment." Pike took a rolled piece of cloth from his saddlebag.

He nodded, and Little Raven led the animal away. Crazy Hawk entered the lodge, with Pike following right behind. Inside, they sat, and Crazy Hawk's wife, Blue Water, served their guest food and coffee. Pike nodded his thanks. Crazy Hawk said something to her in their language and she left.

"If it's important, no need for a woman to hear," the Ute said.

Pike shrugged. It meant little to him if Blue Water listened.

"So, speak, my friend."

Pike tossed him the package. Crazy Hawk raised his eyebrows but untied the thongs holding the cloth roll. He extracted two arrows, then look questioningly at Pike.

"You know who they belong to?"

"I'll look. Too dark in here." Crazy Hawk stood and went outside; dusk had not yet arrived. He was back in a minute or two. "Where'd you get these?"

"My front door."

"What?"

"Somebody shot 'em at me when I went to leave the cabin."

"You know who?"

"If I did, I wouldn't be here talkin' to you and tryin' to find out whose arrows they are, would I?" Pike snapped. "So, do you know? I thought Indians could tell by the markin's or something on arrows."

"I know who it is."

"Then point me in his direction so I can disabuse the son of a bitch of tryin' to kill me."

"I can't do that."

"Why?"

"This is a serious matter."

"Oh, really?" Pike said sarcastically. "Someone trying to kill me is a serious matter? Hell, I didn't realize that."

"This is a serious matter for my people. I can't

just hand over a fellow warrior to you. This calls for much discussion with the people."

"Dammit, I don't want to hear ..."

"This is how it has to be. We discuss it, then tell you the decision. For now, go to Little Raven. I will gather the council."

"I don't like this, Hawk."

"I understand. But if you make a ruckus, you'll be trussed up."

"You try that, and there'll be some dead Utes." Pike's anger was rising fast.

"You'd be dead before you could get those pistols out." Crazy Hawk sighed in frustration. "I don't want that, and I don't want any of my people killed. But we must discuss this."

"Ain't much to discuss, Hawk. The son of a bitch would've killed me if I hadn't turned aside when I did. Just 'cause he didn't succeed doesn't mean he ain't guilty."

"Enough," Crazy Hawk snapped. "This is the way we do things. Different from your people. The council will discuss. We tell you the decision."

"And if I don't like it?"

The Ute shrugged. "You do what you need to. You'll die if you cause trouble, though. Now go to Little Raven. I'll come for you when it's time."

Pike stared at him for some moments, then rose and stormed out, almost tearing the entrance flap free from the tipi. He was only minutely less angry when he called for entrance at Blind Bull's lodge. When he went inside, he said, "Crazy Hawk'll likely be comin' for you directly. Big doin's with the council."

Blind Bull took in Pike's ire and nodded, but he glared at Pike.

The white man said, "I ain't angry enough to hurt Little Raven or any other women."

"Is good." Blind Bull left.

"Come to robes," Little Raven said, tugging on Pike's shirt sleeve.

He shook his head. "No. Not now."

"You not like me anymore?"

"I like you plenty. I just ain't in the mood. I'm too angry to treat you right."

"All right. Come, sit. Coffee?"

"That'd be good." He sat cross-legged near the fire and took the cup of coffee from Little Raven.

"Why you so angry?"

"One of your people tried to kill me."

"No! Why?"

"I don't know. And Crazy Hawk wouldn't tell me who it was." He explained the ambush and the council that was being held.

"All will be right."

"I doubt it. Won't be unless they let me kill the son of a bitch, and I reckon they ain't about to allow that."

Little Raven knelt behind Pike and began kneading his shoulders and back. He felt the anger begin to drain away and patted one of her hands. "You're a good woman, Little Raven." He did not see her smile.

Pike didn't know how long it was before Blind Bull entered the lodge, but it seemed like a long time. "Come," the Ute said. "You too, daughter."

The blood drained from Little Raven's face.

"Why bring her along?" Pike demanded.

"You'll see. Come."

Within minutes, they were entering Many Snows' lodge. The tipi was crowded with warriors and gamey with the odors of sweat, grease, old food, and smoke. It took a few moments for Pike's eyes to get accustomed to the dimness. He glanced around the group of men, and only one held his head down. Got you now, damn you, Pike thought.

Many Snows spoke, with Cray Hawk translating for Pike. "White Shield admits shootin' the arrows at you."

"Good. Now that we know that, hand him over."

Many Snows and Crazy Hawk continued as if Pike had not interrupted. "He says he'll accept punishment from other warriors. Not the white-eye."

"Don't sound reasonable to me, old man. If you won't give him to me, then have him face me one on one. Unless he's a coward."

"He doesn't know about usin' pistols."

"I don't need my shooters to take him on. One against one, me and him, no weapons."

"No!" White Shield shouted, lifting his head for the first time.

"You afraid?" Pike demanded. When the Ute did not answer, he said, "This fella ain't much of a man, Many Snows. You should be ashamed to call him one of your own, a warrior of the Ute people. Shameful."

Many Snows spoke to several of the elders, then asked White Shield something. The latter vigorously shook his head.

"You're right, white-eye," Many Snows said, with

Crazy Hawk translating. "We are ashamed of him."

"So, what now?"

"You go back home. We'll deal with White Shield."

"Not good enough."

"He will be banished. No longer will he be one of the people."

"You send him packin', he'll just try to ambush me again. That wouldn't please me at all."

"We'll see that he doesn't."

Pike didn't believe the old chief. There was, he thought, no way to keep White Shield from trying to kill him again once they cast him out of the village. Suddenly he asked, "Why'd you bring Little Raven here?"

The woman had been trying to hide behind Pike and next to Blind Bull.

"She's the reason for White Shield's attack on you."

"What?"

"White Shield wanted Little Raven. He was angry when she went with you."

Pike cranked his head around. "Did you know about this?"

She shook her head vigorously, her long hair whipping back and forth, mostly covering her frightened eyes.

"Do you want him?" Pike asked.

"No! Want you!" Certainty was strong in her voice.

"Still want to just banish him and let him take another run at me, Many Snows?" Pike asked.

Before the chief could answer, White Shield shouted, "No!" He jumped up, pulled his knife from the sheath at his waist, and tried to leap across the fire at Pike.

Crazy Hawk, standing next to Pike, shoved the white man out of the way. He blocked White Shield's knife arm with his left and plunged his own knife into White Shield's chest. The former fell into the fire and was quickly pulled out by several warriors.

"You didn't need to do that, Hawk. I would've taken him down."

"I know. Better one of us does it than an outsider. Now go, take Little Raven back to her lodge. Let her know you want her as much as she says she wants you." His face, which had hardened at the killing of White Shield, softened a little. When Pike hesitated, the Ute said, "You'll be safe here. Anyone who was friends with White Shield will do nothing against you. They are ashamed."

A rumble of agreement rippled around the lodge. Pike nodded and left with Little Raven.

CHAPTER 15

Pike suspected he was far more shocked than Little Raven was when he slapped her. He stood for a few moments, almost shaking with anger at himself, then spun and ran out of the lodge. He ran to his horse, jumped on, and raced away.

At his cabin, he leaped off the mare and let her wander on her own, not caring. Inside, he frantically searched for the small bottle of whiskey he kept should a need for celebration arose. He had hid it so the Utes would not find it, and in his rage he was unsure of where he had hidden. He rarely drank, and when he did, he restricted himself to one or two belts, but tonight called for more than a couple of shots. It called for draining at least one bottle. He would use the redeye to expunge the memory and the shame of what he had just done.

He finally found it in an extra coffeepot and pulled it out. Flopping down on one of his wooden chairs, he pulled the cork out and downed nearly half the bottle in one long swallow, then burped.

Taking another smaller swig, he cursed himself for being so angry at Little Raven for something so minor. Well, he wasn't really angry at Little Raven; she was just the unfortunate victim when his rage exploded.

A warrior named Red Scar had taunted him for much of the evening, trying to goad him into a fight. For reasons Pike did not know, the Ute hated him and wanted an excuse to kill him. With his anger rising, Pike looked at Crazy Hawk several times. Finally, the Ute nodded, indicating he could go ahead and fight Red Scar. Pike rose and took off his gun belt as the people gathered in a circle. He handed it to Many Snows and flipped his Bowie so it stuck in the ground.

Red Scar smirked and drew his knife in one hand, his tomahawk in the other.

"No weapons," Pike snapped.

Crazy Hawk said something in his own language. Red Scar hesitated, then with a scowl, he tossed his weapons to the ground.

Both men moved forward. Red Scar was a fairly big man, outweighing Pike by at least a dozen pounds. He looked flabby, Pike thought, though he would not underestimate the man's strength.

The two charged at each other, slamming together and latching on, straining to gain a grip. Suddenly Red Scar got a foot behind Pike's leg and shoved, knocking the bounty hunter to his back and landing on top of him.

"Damn," Pike mumbled. He tried to avoid Red Scar's fist but was only partially successful, and the blow caught a good section of his cheek. His head rang, but he managed to slam a forearm across Red Scar's mouth and push the warrior off him.

The combatants regained their feet, breathing heavily. They charged each other again, but in the eyeblink before they collided, Pike dropped to one knee. Red Scar ran into Pike's shoulder, and he rose and pushed the Ute over it. The Indian landed with a thud in the dirt.

Pike tried to stomp on Red Scar's chest, but the Ute grabbed his foot and, despite his labored breathing, twisted it and shoved Pike away. Red Scar rose, and the two men watched each other warily, then once more, they charged. The Ute tried to gouge out Pike's right eye, but the white man managed to jerk his head out of the way and the finger hit his forehead. Pike latched his teeth onto Red Scar's nose. The Ute bellowed and shoved Pike away.

"That's enough," Blind Bull said in English, then repeated it in his language.

With a glare, Red Scar turned and kicked dirt all over Pike's Colts.

Pike's eyes blazed as his anger spiked. He went to charge the Ute again, but Blind Bull and Crazy Hawk grabbed his arms and held him. He struggled as Red Scar smirked.

Blind Bull said something in Ute to his fellow tribesman, and Red Scar wiped the sneer off his face and shoved his way through the cloud of people, angry.

"Calm down, Brodie," Crazy Hawk said. "He won't cause you any more trouble. Me and my father will see to that."

"Let me go," Pike snarled.

The two Utes hesitated for a moment, then nodded to each other and released his arms.

Pike grabbed his gun belt and fastened it around his waist, picked up his Bowie and sheathed it, and stormed into the lodge he shared with Little Raven. He plopped down. "Food, woman," he snapped.

With a worried look, she hurriedly filled a bowl with elk stew, but when she bent to hand it to him, she stumbled and spilled the hot food over his shoulder and into his lap. Little Raven, sorry about what she had done, stood frozen. Before she could even try to apologize, Pike bellowed and jumped up, and without thinking, he slapped her. She fell back a step, looking at him in shock. Pike glanced at his hand as if he had never seen it before, then spun and raced out. He ran to his horse, which was saddled nearby, leapt on, and rode hell-bent for leather out of the village.

In his cabin, he condemned himself for his action, his sudden departure from decency, his life. He pitied and scorned himself. He poured more liquor down his throat, not tasting it but feeling its heat burn deep inside him, igniting more flames of self-loathing.

He drained the bottle, surprised it was gone already. "Hell and damnation," he snapped. He flung the bottle against the wall, where it shattered. "Damn you, Brodie Pike!" he roared. "Damn you to hell and back!"

The redeye sparked an unrestrained flame of

anger. He leaped up hand and stormed around the room, tossing or smashing anything he could grab while spewing curses in a rage-filled rant.

It was not long before he ran out of steam and fell into a chair, gasping for breath, chest heaving, sight blurred, hands shaking.

Before long, he was asleep, his snoring loud and ragged. His dreams were dark and disturbing, and he growled and mumbled curses as he jerked and fidgeted. He shook so hard at one point that he fell off the chair. Lying on the floor, barely conscious, he wondered how he had gotten there, then decided he didn't care. He slipped back into sleep again, the nightmares no less disturbing—visions of the fires of hell burning all around him, of Ute women coming for him with knives in their hands, and of Ute warriors chasing him, intent on scalping him. He tossed and turned, jerking about.

He rose when his gorge told him the poison was climbing inside him and managed to stumble outside. Holding the corner of the cabin, he bent and poured out the contents of his stomach. He stood that way for some time until the retching dwindled and finally stopped. He remained there, breathing heavily. Then he heard the voice.

"I came to punish you, but you're doin' a good enough job yourself," Crazy Hawk said.

"Go to hell, Hawk," Pike growled.

"I go when my time comes. Not before." Crazy Hawk sounded gleeful.

Pike retched again, but his stomach was empty.

"You look like you're havin' fun, so finish what

you're doing here," Crazy Hawk said cheerfully. "I make coffee." He went inside the cabin and stopped when he saw the mess. Shaking his head, he grabbed some wood, stoked the fire, and put some coffee on to heat.

Before long, Pike wobbled in and sank into a chair.

"You have much work to clean the place up."

"Maybe. Maybe not. I might just burn it down and everything in it."

"You won't do that."

"Don't be so sure."

"You like it here. You'll stay, fix the place up." Crazy Hawk set a mug of coffee in front of Pike, who nodded his thanks. "What made you do what you did?"

"I was angry. Red Scar kicked dirt all over my revolvers. Those pieces are special to me, and I can't abide anyone abusin' 'em, so I went to my lodge before I did something that might set the other warriors, includin' you and your pa, on me, maybe even kill me. I hoped to calm down. Then Little Raven spilled hot stew on me. Almost scalded my pecker, dammit." He shivered at the memory. "I just lost my reason for a moment." He shook his head in disgust.

Crazy Hawk said nothing.

"You said you came to punish me?" Pike asked in wonder. "Why? You've been known to lodgepole your woman."

"My wife and my sister are different."

"Like hell. If you can beat your woman, I can beat mine." He almost choked on the words. If he had not done what he did, he would never have believed he could do such a thing. He never had, and he'd figured he never would. Having done so sickened him, but his reasoning would make no sense to Crazy Hawk.

"Maybe you're right, so I leave you alone."

"Damn good thing. I'd hate to have to kill you now."

"Don't think you can in your condition."

"Maybe you're right, but I'd be glad to give it a try if you want to prove I can't."

"I'd kill you for sure."

"I really don't care."

"You're loco, my friend."

"Could very well be." He paused and sighed. "When you get back to the village, tell Little Raven I'm powerful sorry for what I did. And tell her I'll never bother her again."

"I will tell her." The warrior strolled out.

Pike looked around at the devastation in the room, then shrugged. "Oh, to hell with it," he mumbled and flopped onto his bed. Sleep didn't take long to arrive, but it was no more peaceful than it had been earlier.

The room didn't look any better in the morning, nor did he feel much better. He managed to heat up some coffee and down it, then got another cup. He had just taken a sip when a knock came at the door. Unlike he usually did, he left his guns in their holsters when he answered the door. He figured that if it was someone who wanted to kill him, he would not object.

For the second time in less than twenty-four hours, he was surprised. "What're you doin' here,

Raven?" he asked when he was able to find his voice, wincing at the bruise on her cheek.

"I come in?" she asked in reply.

"Um, well, sure." He stepped back and let her into the cabin. He was embarrassed by the mess, but she showed no reaction. "Why are you here?" he repeated.

"I come to clean up mess. Crazy Hawk said it very bad. Seems like."

"Why are you willin' to do that?"

"It is the way of things. Men make messes, woman clean 'em up." She shrugged. It was the view she had of life, and nothing would change it.

"After what I did?"

"You discipline bad wife."

"What? No, no, that ain't right. You're a good woman, and a decent man doesn't hit a good woman—or any woman."

"White-eyes maybe like that, but not the People. A Ute woman who spills hot food on husband deserves punishment. You punished me, as was right. It over now. I clean up, you come back to village, all be good again."

He shook his head in wonder. "You sure?"

"Yes."

"What about Red Scar?"

"He not bother you. Crazy Hawk and Blind Bull will make sure."

"I ain't so sure. And I ain't so sure I deserve forgiveness after what I did."

"Hush. You go clean up now. You stink of bad whiskey and stomach spillings. I make breakfast," she added merrily when a grimace at the very thought of food crossed his face. Then she grinned. "I not spill it on you. Then I clean up here while you fix broken things."

"Yes'm," Pike said humbly as he gathered fresh clothes and headed outside to where he kept a barrel of water and a basin to wash, shave, and change.

CHAPTER 16

Pike fervently wished he had not heard the sounds. But he had, even above the jolting and creaking of the wagon, and they told him that something unpleasant was happening just ahead. He wanted to turn and drive off, ignoring them, but he couldn't, not without finding out what was happening. He moved on slowly and stopped the wagon with the muzzle of the mule sticking into the glade just off the trail. The scene was as bad as he had feared.

An old squaw was on the ground, and a man was just finishing his ghastly business on her. An old warrior was hanging by his wrists, feet barely touching the ground, from a cottonwood a few yards from where his wife—Pike assumed the unfortunate woman was his wife—was being abused. He was bloody and appeared to be barely alive.

Another burst of hooting and reprehensible laughter—the foul sounds that had warned Pike of evil doings but had drawn him—burst forth from the man, who was buttoning his trousers as another began loosening his in preparation for replacing him. Two others watched as the new man knelt between the old squaw's legs.

Pike cursed silently but fervently and efficiently as he slid off the wagon seat and stalked toward the group, pulling a pistol as he did. He did not hesitate. He simply blew out the fornicator's brains with a quick shot to the head, then blasted the just-finished rapist with a shot to the heart.

The other two men gasped and went for their holstered six-shooters, but they had no chance against Pike and soon lay dead on the grass.

Pike slipped his pistol away, swept up a blanket near the fire, and knelt to gently cover the woman. "They won't bother you no more," he said, feeling stupid for offering the useless platitude but having no other words that would suffice.

He rose, hurried to the tree, and cut the ropes holding the old warrior, who was in poor shape but not as bad as Pike had thought he was. Still, he had to hold onto the man to keep him from falling. He let the warrior rest for a few moments, then helped him over and eased him down next to his wife.

The Indians clutched each other, crying in their fear and shame.

Pike stood uneasily. He still had no words for these two unfortunate folks. Finally, he asked, "You have people nearby who can look after you?"

The old man looked up and stared at him a few moments. The tears had stopped, but the shame at having been unable to protect himself and his woman—and the knowledge that getting revenge for being wronged would have been beyond him even had this stranger not come along—remained. Then a blankness dropped over his eyes and he nodded. "Two, three miles." He jerked his head toward the southeast.

"You gonna be able to get to them?"

The warrior nodded once and jerked his head in the direction of the two Indian ponies nearby, one with a travois sparsely laden with supplies.

"You with Many Snows' band?"

"Have small village near his."

Pike nodded. He wandered over and looked at the two animals. They were serviceable, but barely. He got one of the dead men's horses and carefully loaded the packages from the travois on that horse, then returned to the old couple. He knelt and easily but gently swept the woman up. Fear raced across her face. Pike gave her what he hoped was a reassuring smile. "I won't harm you, Grandmother," he said quietly, using the term of respect he had learned from Little Raven.

She relaxed a little under his friendly look and his use of the honorific.

Pike carried her to the travois and laid her tenderly on it. He began to lay a blanket across her but stopped when he felt the man's hand on his shoulder.

"I do," the warrior said. He looked a bit stronger now than he had when Pike cut him down from the tree a few minutes ago.

Pike nodded and rose. He strode across the glade and pulled his wagon toward the miscreants' fire.

Within minutes, he had unceremoniously thrown the four bodies into the bed of his small-box farm wagon. Then he tied their remaining horses next to his at the back of the wagon. He climbed onto the conveyance's hard wooden seat and glanced at the warrior, who stood watching him, ready to mount his pony. Pike waved.

"What's your name?" the old Ute called.

"Brodie Pike."

"Thank you, Brodie Pike. I am Fallen Timber."

Even at this distance, Pike thought he could see both pride and irony on the old man's face. He tipped his hat and rode off, paying no attention to the gruesome cargo bouncing in the wagon bed behind him.

Just after noon, Pike rode into Skeeter Creek and pulled his mule to s stop in front of the town marshal's office. The man who came out wearing the star was not the same one Pike had met on his previous visits to the town. He briefly wondered what had happened to the other but realized he didn't care.

"You responsible for all this?" the lawman asked as he looked into the wagon bed. He pulled up the head of one of the men by the hair. "Hey, that's Luke Stumpert." He grabbed another. "And Rafe Biggins, Barny Weathers, and Ox Utley," he added after checking the others.

"Friends of yours?" Pike asked dryly.

"I knew 'em, that's a fact. But you didn't answer my question. You responsible for these men bein' dead?"

"Reckon so."

"What in hell ever possessed you to kill four men?" He didn't seem angry as much as full of curiosity about what had brought on the bloodbath.

"Caught 'em abusin' an old couple back down the trail a little way. Didn't seem like a good thing for them to be doin'."

"Old couple? Ain't no old couple livin' down the trail that way that I know of."

"Couple Indians. Utes. Ancient warrior and his squaw."

"And you killed four white men in cold blood for abusin' a couple broken-down Indians?" The marshal was incredulous.

"Cold blood, my ass," Pike snapped. "Indians or not, they were old, feeble, and defenseless. Didn't seem too mannerly to me for four strong, healthy men to hang an old man from a tree and torture him while at the same time ... hell, you can't even call what they were doin' to that old woman fornicatin'. It was god-awful and sickening. Shameful." The rage he had felt when he had first seen the site swelled back up in him, and he fought to force it down.

"Ain't many folks 'round here likely to think the same."

"Then they're as bad as these four. And it don't matter none to me what they might think."

The lawman stood staring up at Pike for a bit, still baffled by his actions. Then he shook his head. "Reckon it was Dead Wood and his ol' squaw."

"I believe his name is Fallen Timber."

"Right. Folks here nicknamed him 'Dead Wood.'

Kind of a play on his name."

"A playful lot they must be." He looked around. "Be obliged if you'd check to see if these four devils were wanted."

"You a bounty hunter?"

"I have been. At times."

"Now?"

"Haven't been at it in a spell, but if there's a bounty on 'em, I figure the cash is mine."

"Mercenary bastard, ain't you?"

"Nope. Just practical." He chucked a thumb at the bodies. "I'll drop these off at the undertaker's if you got one. Or a doc's if you'd rather. If you got neither, I'll dump 'em anywhere."

"Take 'em down the street here to the livery stable. Just leave 'em. I'll have someone take 'em over to Abercrombie's funeral home one at a time so he's not overwhelmed."

Pike nodded. "I'll be in town tonight. Stayin' at the Creek Inn." He had considered another night at Evangeline's, but his closeness to Little Raven these days made that seem wrong, and his anger at these four villains had not left him in a lighthearted mood. "I'll be pullin' out tomorrow after I get what supplies I come after. I expect to have payment in hand on these men before I leave."

He had known by the look on the lawman's face when he said he knew them that the dead men were, indeed, outlaws.

"Don't know if I'll have time to ..." The marshal clamped his mouth shut, knowing his mouth had moved a lot faster than his brain. He had figured on stalling long enough for Pike to leave town so he could collect the bounty himself, but it was too late now. He figured he could drum up a fair amount of cash on the horses, the tack, and whatever else the men had on them. "Hey, wait a minute, mister. There's four men here and only three horses, figurin' one of the four tied to your wagon is yours. Where's the other one?"

"Probably in a Ute village by now. Or it will be soon."

"Damn redskin. Always knew he was a horse thief."

"That old man ain't a horse thief. He needed another horse, and these fellas didn't need theirs no longer, so I gave one to him. If you want someone to point a finger at, you'll have to point it at me—but if you do, you just might lose that finger. I don't much cotton to havin' fingers pointed at me, even by some punk wearin' a tin star."

He hauled the wagon away from the hitching rail and drove slowly down the street.

Butch Davies, the liveryman, who generally was friendly toward Pike, didn't seem thrilled to have a wagonload of bodies in his stable, but he was mollified by the possibility that he could earn some extra money once the bodies were removed. "Just remember which horse is mine and treat her accordingly," Pike warned as he left.

"You know I do, and I will," Davies said, affronted.

Pike simply nodded.

** ** ** ** **

Pike was loading the wagon in the morning when the marshal strode up. "You were right," the lawman said. "There were circulars on those boys." He held out some greenbacks. "Two hundred for the lot of 'em."

Pike set down the box of canned goods he had been carrying and turned to the marshal. Instead of taking the money, he cast a baleful glare on the lawman, who held the stare for a few moments, then blinked. He reached into his shirt pocket and pulled out more bills. "Sorry. I got confused," he mumbled. "It was two hundred each."

"That sounds about right." Pike took the money and counted it, then folded the bills in half and stuck the pile in a pocket. "Don't fret, Marshal. You'll make this much or more sellin' the horses and all their gear."

The marshal grunted, then asked, "Leavin' soon?"

"Eager to get rid of me?"

"No, that ain't it," the man said.

"You're as bad a liar as you are a lawman."

"Mighty rude thing to say."

"It's the truth, and the truth hurts when it slaps you in the face. If you were a competent lawman, you would've brought those boys to justice a long time ago and collected the bounty yourself. Of course, it could be that you're not incompetent but were in cahoots with those scum. That might explain why you never did anything about them." Pike's voice had turned harsh. He was tired of dealing with this fool.

The marshal's face darkened and his hand inched toward his holstered six-gun, but it stopped at the steely look in Pike's eyes. "Just get yourself out of Skeeter Creek fast," he muttered before stomping off.

Pike watched the lawman for a moment, annoyed and now concerned. He was not afraid of the marshal, but he was sure the lawman was going to get a group together and ambush him on the road. "I'll be damned if I'll let that happen," he muttered as he turned back to his work.

Less than an hour later, Pike clattered out of town at a leisurely pace, his riding horse tied to the back of the wagon. A half-mile outside town he picked up speed, but not too much. He figured the lawman and the men he'd bring with him would wait until nightfall, so they would be in no rush to catch up to him. Still, he did want to put some distance between him and whoever might follow him.

CHAPTER 17

Five miles or so down the road, Pike pulled onto the hidden track Crazy Hawk had shown him. He had used it only once after that first trip, not having felt the need to, but he was certain that men from Skeeter Creek were planning to follow him.

He pushed on farther than normal, skipping the cave he usually used and making for the large one about midway along the trail. It was near dark, and Pike hurriedly unhitched the wagon, led the two animals to the rear of the spacious cave, and tended them. Afterward, he tossed some hay and a bit of the grain he carried in the wagon to the animals. Only then did he light a fire and make himself a small supper. Sleep came soon after.

In the morning, he had another small meal and some coffee. Then, before he hitched up the wagon, he went to a small cave within the cave and pulled his sniper rifle out of the dark crevice he had stored it in on his last journey on the buffalo trail. He had been worried that when he was away on these trips, someone might stumble on the house and discover the valuable weapon, so he had stored it here. To protect it, he had wrapped it in a long piece of buffalo hide, fur on, then three layers of canvas tarp, then another piece of buffalo hide, the bundle bound with thin strips of rawhide. He decided it had not been tampered with and slid it back into the almost-impossible-to-see fissure.

Finally, he hitched the mule to the wagon, tied his horse to the rear, kicked out the last of the small fire, and pressed on. He spent another night on the back road but then made a long push, driving straight through instead of camping where the road crossed the far end of his meadow.

It was full dark when he arrived at the house, but he forced himself to unload the wagon and tend to the animals before he flopped on his bed of buffalo robes. In the morning, he put all his goods away before making some repairs to the wagon.

** ** ** ** **

Crazy Hawk and Little Raven rode up one afternoon, much to Pike's delight. Pike made them some chicken, which both Utes thought less than tasty and poorly cooked. But they ate it, grimacing the whole time.

"You tryin' to kill us, Brodie?" Crazy Hawk said with a wry grin. "What is this? Buzzard?"

"It's chicken."

"Good to know so I can avoid it for all time."

"Hmmph," Pie said. "Raven likes it. Don't you, woman?"

"Is good," she said tentatively, not wanting to hurt his feelings, then added quietly, "Not very."

Crazy Hawk laughed.

"It's the last time I'll feed you chicken ..."

"That's a relief."

"... or anything else."

They spent some time afterward sipping coffee, and Pike's annoyance slowly disappeared, replaced by a desire for Little Raven.

"Fallen Timber says you saved him and Light Elk from some evil men."

"Just happened to be where I needed to be to discourage some bastards from doin' more deviltry than they had already done."

"The old man says you killed four men. White men. To save a couple old Utes."

Pike shrugged, embarrassed.

"Ain't many white-eyes'd do that for red people."

"Didn't see Indians, just a couple old folks bein' sorely abused. I didn't like it. Never have."

"Well, my people're grateful. Fallen Timber says he wants to see you."

"What in hell for?"

"Give a feast in your honor." Crazy Hawk grinned.

"That ain't necessary."

"It'd be an insult to him and to all Utes not to accept."

"That true?" Pike asked Little Raven.

"Yes."

"Damn. Well, I reckon I'll visit then soon." His eyes flicked to Little Raven, then to the robes, then to Crazy Hawk.

The warrior was astute enough to pick up on the hint. He stood and stretched. "I'll sleep outside," he said and headed out.

Pike and Little Raven were rolling in the robes moments later, hungry for each other.

** ** ** ** **

Not long after they left Pike's cabin, Pike said, "This ain't the way to your village, Hawk."

"Nope. Fallen Timber has a smaller village a few miles from ours."

Pike nodded. "He said he had a small village near where I found 'em. He an outcast or something? Banished like Many Snows wanted to do with White Shield?"

"Nope. He just likes it that way. Like I told you, most of us live in small villages, just a few families. He has four families includin' his own in his village. He was a great warrior, one of the bravest. Besides, he likes bein' chief of his own clan."

"You folks ever have contact with each other?"

"Yep. All the time. They visit us, we visit them. My wife, Blue Water, is from Fallen Timber's band. His daughter in fact."

"The way we're headin' will take us closer to Skeeter Creek than your village."

"Yep, but not all that much. Fallen Timber and Light Elk go there at times to get supplies."

"I don't expect they're treated very well after what I've seen in that town."

"Nope. But it's the only place they think they can get some of the things they need. Reckon it's true, but Many Snows says we don't need those things, so we stay clear of that damned place."

"You sound disappointed," Pike said, surprised.

"Not about goin' to town. Wish we could wipe the place out, though. People livin' there is just another way of pushin' us off our land." His voice had turned bitter.

Pike had no response to that, so he rode in silence for a bit, then asked, "Where'd you learn to speak English?"

"Blind Bull sent me to the Los Piños Agency when I was younger. Wanted me to get educated."

"Education's a good thing, but you don't sound like you agree."

"Didn't mind the education. Figured it'd help us all when the white-eyes come to take over all our land." His anger was rising. "What I didn't like was them tellin' me I had to learn farmin' or some other trade. Didn't set well with me, so I left after a couple years. Didn't take much to farmin' or white man's clothes, but I did learn to speak your language."

"Damn well, too."

By late afternoon, they arrived at a small village. The three stopped in front of Fallen Timber's tipi, where the old man waited, trying to look dignified, though the shame in his ancient eyes made it difficult. They dismounted, and Little Raven began leading the horses away.

"Fallen Timber, this is the white-eye who helped you and Light Elk that day."

"I remember," he said in broken English, voice trembling with the humiliation of meeting this man in front of the others.

"You understand English?" Pike asked.

"Some."

"Good." Not knowing if what he was about to do was improper, Pike ignored the gasps behind him and the drawing of weapons and laid his hands gently on the old man's shoulders. "You have no reason to be ashamed, Grandfather," he said quietly. "You couldn't do much at that time because you were ambushed. It wasn't like you was prepared for them. You couldn't fight well."

"You killed them all. No trouble." The shame still shook him to his core.

"I surprised them just like they did you. I killed 'em before they even knew I was there. Same as you were surprised, and they grabbed you. If they knew I was comin', they would've abused me, too. You can't fight folks you don't know are there."

A little life and light came into Falling Timber's cloudy eyes. After some moments, he said, "You a good man, white-eye."

Pike grinned. "My name's Brodie, remember?" He removed his hands from Fallen Timber's shoulders after a brief squeeze.

He turned to Light Elk, who was standing behind the chief and a little to the side. Her head was hanging. He lifted her chin with a finger. "And you, Grandmother, should not be ashamed either." He didn't know if she understood him, then he heard Crazy Hawk translating quietly. "You could not do anything against those bad men. You are a strong woman who endured much, yet you are still able to care for your man and keep his lodge well for all to see."

Tears started streaming down her creased face.

Not knowing or caring if it was improper, he gathered the tiny, frail woman in his arms and stroked her hair for a few moments before releasing her.

A man stepped up and gently tugged Pike's sleeve. When Pike had turned to face him, he said, "I'm Panther, Fallen Timber's son. You unusual."

"Not really."

Panther started to say something else, but Pike held up his hand to stop him. Over his shoulder, he said, "Hawk, tell these people to stop treatin' me special or whatever they think they're doin'."

"They respect you, Brodie. They honor you for havin' saved their chief. Accept their gratitude, my friend."

"Yes," agreed Little Raven, who had come up beside him.

"Bah. You said there was gonna be a feast. Let's get to it. I'm hungry, and it'll take these folks' minds off embarrassin' me."

Crazy Hawk laughed, then said something in Ute, and suddenly the little village was a beehive of activity. A central fire was built up, and women started bringing out food: slices of elk and buffalo to be roasted or grilled over the fire, thin stews of the same meats with a variety of vegetables, bread made of ground corn, and a few things Pike did not want to contemplate. Soon the food was being passed around.

Crazy Hawk had a tough time translating for everyone as the Utes peppered Pike with questions and he replied.

After everyone was sated on the food and coffee, Panther and his young son, Red Quiver, began drumming, and the Utes started to dance. Pike watched in good humor as Crazy Hawk finally got around to naming the people: Pretty Robe, Panther's wife, and Lazy Calf, their daughter; Running Fire, Panther's oldest son, Porcupine, his wife, and Winter Sky, their daughter; Black Knife, his wife, White Smoke, and Braided Horn, their son.

Winter Sky and Braided Horn, both around eleven or twelve, Pike figured, had seen few white men and none this close. After some tentativeness, they grew bolder and began tugging playfully on Pike's long, drooping mustache, giggling as he fiercely fake-growled at them.

He spent a couple of days with Falling Timber's band and thought again how strange it was that he had become comfortable around these people who were in many ways very different from him. On the other hand, they were like any other people in most things.

He, Crazy Hawk, and Little Raven left then, with Pike having an invitation to visit any time he desired. In the weeks after, he took advantage of that, enjoying talking with the men, though that was sometimes tricky since none of them had a great command of the other's language, and playing with the two young children. He hunted with them at times, easily bringing down elk with his Winchester and being impressed when they brought down one of the big animals with arrows.

He also spent time in Many Snows' village, swapping tales of their great deeds with the men and sharing the robes with Little Raven. The Ute woman also visited him at his house at times, where they would enjoy the solitude with each other.

Because of these pleasant times, he began to think that his idea of being away from humanity—well, white folks anyway—might not be such a good idea. He could, he thought, be happy here. He smiled. All he had to do was figure out what he could do to earn a living.

CHAPTER 18

Hate roared up inside Brodie Pike like the powerful eruption of the giant geyser he had seen once up north as he looked at the devastation in the small Ute camp. Hate for the evil men who had laid waste to the village of only four lodges, and even more intense hate for himself for having been the cause of it.

It was always thus for him. He should have learned years ago. He had known for a long time that he was trouble for his fellow man. He forgot all the good he had done; it never entered his mind, only the bad. Try as he might, he could never be of true help to anyone. Always—always—he left despair, destruction, and death behind when all he had wanted was to bring good. He had made up his mind after being duped by Pony Stallings in Arrowhead that he would find an out-of-the-way place and retire from bounty hunting, and pretty much everything else. But once again, he had failed to keep his word to himself to keep away from people. No, he had taken the Utes into his heart, and they in turn had taken him into theirs. By doing so, he had brought death and disaster upon these people.

No, never again, he vowed. That was if he lived through it all. His death would make moot any possibility of him going back on his word, and he thought that might be for the best. He only hoped the Utes would let him get his revenge before they killed the man who had brought this catastrophe to their land and people.

He sat on his horse where the trail entered the small meadow between two short, sheer bluffs, looking at the forlorn scene. The four lodges were still smoking, what was left of them. A few of the lodgepole pines that had held up the buffalo-hide coverings stood starkly against the green backdrop of the cottonwoods and aspens.

Fighting down his rising bile, Pike dismounted and began walking slowly toward the remains of the nearest lodge. He found Black knife and his twelve-year-old son, Braided Horn, first. Since their knives were still sheathed, Pike figured they had been caught unaware and shot in the back. It was only later, Pike was certain, that they had been scalped and mutilated. The initial shots would have alerted the rest of the camp. A few yards away, he came upon the body of Red Quiver. The almost-teenager must have heard the gunfire, come to see what was happening, and run right into a fusillade of bullets. Despite the blood, Pike saw at least five holes in the boy's shirt.

Farther along, in front of the smoldering remains

of a lodge, lay its owner Panther, the father of Red Quiver. His shirt had several bullet holes too, but judging by the bloody tomahawk in the arm that had been almost severed among the other indignities visited on his body, he must have wounded at least one of the attackers.

With deepening dread, he pushed on. It was as bad as he had expected. Running Fire, Panther's older son, and the aging Fallen Timber were the last line of defense. They had been caught, tortured, and forced to watch the depredations, then killed, scalped, and mutilated.

The females had fared even worse. Light Elk, Fallen Timber's elderly wife, had been gutted like a fish, though for some reason, Pike thought she had not been seriously molested. The attackers, he was sure, had reserved that for the younger females: Panther's wife, Pretty Robe, and daughter, Lazy Calf, and Running Fire's wife, Porcupine. He suddenly stood stock-still; two were missing, Black Knife's wife, White Smoke, and Panther's eleven-year-old daughter, Winter Sky.

"Sweet Jumpin' Jesus," he murmured. "They've been taken." He hesitated for a moment, then headed for his horse. Crazy Hawk and Blind Bull would somehow learn about this soon enough, and they would bury their dead clansmen and women. Right now, he had to try to get the woman and the girl back if he could. In seconds, he had mounted and was racing down the trail.

He found Winter Sky a little over a half-hour later. He had been riding hard, then suddenly stopped, something tugging at his mind. He turned back and moved slowly back down the trail, then stopped again, listening. The sound that had caught his subconscious came again—a low, pained groan.

"Damn," he muttered as he dismounted and hurried into the pines. The girl lay, naked, mostly on her left side in a small clearing, moaning softly in agony.

Pike knelt next to Winter Sky and shook his head in pity and fury. Her naked back and buttocks were scraped raw, and the oozing wounds were covered with dirt. He gently pulled her onto her back, knowing it would hurt even more but needing to see how badly she was injured on the other side. As expected, she screeched as the dirt and pebbles gouged deeper into the seeping abrasions on her back.

Winter Sky had been abused unmercifully, and her body was covered with bruises as well as blood from numerous small knife wounds. One deep furrow traced a ragged course from just below her bellybutton to curve around her just-beginning-to-bud right breast. She was close to death.

Winter Sky's eyelids suddenly fluttered open, then widened with fear.

"It's okay, Winter Sky," he said soothingly. "You know me."

"But you are like ..." she moaned.

"No, I ain't like the white men who did this to you. You know that after all the times I visited with you and the others. Those men will pay for what they done, I promise you. Now, first thing is to get you back to your folks ... ah, your people to get you some help."

"No. I dead. Almost. Want to die."

Pike picked up one of her tiny hands in both his large ones. "I can get you back to your people, and you'll get better," he said, not convincing even to himself. He gazed at her, trying not to see the damage that had been done to her not-yet-womanly body, but it was evident that she had suffered immensely and lost a lot of blood. What had been done to her mind was as bad, if not worse.

"No. I hurt. Am dying. You kill me. Take pain away. I go to ancestors in Spirit World."

"That won't make your auntie White Smoke very happy when I find her."

"She escaped. Ran away to tell Blind Bull and the others. She safe."

"You sure?"

"Yes." Her voice was barely a whisper, but it grew stronger as she spoke. "Now you help me to the Spirit World."

"I can't do that, Winter Sky. I'll get you help, and you'll be all right."

Her eyes closed again, and she weakly shook her head. Pike remained kneeling by her side, wondering what to do. Never had he faced such a dilemma. Killing this girl was unthinkable, but he knew there truly was no help for her. He had to choose between doing as she wished and ending her suffering quickly and almost painlessly or kneeling at her side, holding her hand until she expired on her own. That was unthinkable too, considering the tremendous agony she was in.

He sighed, rage and disgust fighting for supremacy inside him. Keeping her hand in his left, he used the right to pull out his knife. He took a deep breath to settle himself, then let it out slowly as he plunged the blade into her heart.

Winter Sky's eyes popped open, fear and pain bright in them, but after a moment, they softened into serenity. She smiled, then she was gone.

Pike continued kneeling beside her for some time, holding the dead girl's hand. At one point, he wondered why drops of water were appearing on her skin, then realized they were his tears. He did not care that he was crying.

When he finally rose, it was with a heavy heart and a leaden disposition. He considered burying her here but decided that was not right. She belonged with her people. Revenge could wait a little longer. He got the extra blanket he carried with his bedroll and carefully wrapped Winter Sky in it. Gritting his teeth, he slung her small, light body over his shoulder so he could mount his horse.

Even though he knew the girl could not feel anything, Pike rode slowly, not wanting to jar her corpse. He was aware that that was foolish, but he figured she had suffered enough indignities in life that he would not make her suffer any more in death.

As he rode, he let the rage inside him fester and simmer, hot enough to keep the fire burning but not enough to make him explode. No, he would save the fury for when he found the animals who had done this and make them pay.

Pike had given up the religion of his youth—indeed, all religion—when he saw the inhumanity and incalculable suffering during the war, but now a touch of it back to him in a pained and resentful manner. "Lord Almighty, for once, won't you let me be the one who suffers instead of these innocent people? Dammit, why would you let this happen to a child and others who were no danger to the whites in Skeeter Creek?"

It took him far longer to get back to the camp than it had to find the girl. When he arrived, he eased Winter Sky down next to Porcupine, her mother. Then he went about moving the other bodies as gently as he could, laying them neatly in front of the remains of their lodges.

He was almost finished when Blind Bull, Crazy Hawk, and a dozen other warriors thundered into the camp. Four warriors immediately nocked arrows, ready to drill him. Pike straightened, not reaching for his Colts, just waiting. If they killed him, so be it, he figured. His only regret would be not getting revenge.

"No!" Crazy Hawk shouted. "What happened, Brodie?"

"Don't know for sure," Pike growled through gritted teeth. "Place was mostly like this when I got here."

"Mostly like this?"

"Bodies were scattered all over. White Smoke and Winter Sky were missing. I went searching for them. Found the girl much abused. Before she died, she told me White Smoke had gotten away and was headin' toward your village to tell you."

"She did," Blind Bull said, his deep voice a raging rumble.

"I brought Winter Sky back here and started to arrange the bodies so they could have what little dignity was possible."

One of the warriors with a nocked bow, Red Scar, said something in his language.

"He said we should kill you now," Crazy Hawk translated.

"I know what he said. If it'll make you folks feel better to do so, have at it. But it'd be damned foolish."

"Why?"

"How're you gonna avenge the deaths of these people? Attack Skeeter Creek? That'd only get the rest of your clan killed, and for nothin'. I can move around the town easy, though I figure I'll do more ambushin' than wanderin' through town shootin' folks. These people here," he said, waving his hand at the bodies, "deserve vengeance. And by God, I will see that they get it." He realized tears were again streaming down his face.

"He lies," Red Scar said. "Look, he cries like a woman. He not want us to kill him. He afraid."

Before anyone could say anything, Blind Bull edged his pony over to Red Scar, then smacked the warrior across the face with his bow, almost knocking him off his horse.

"How'll you do that?" Crazy Hawk asked.

"Don't know yet. Ain't had time to think about it. But I'll get it done."

"Can we trust you?" another warrior, Three Elk,

asked. "You're a white-eye, and white-eyes did this."

"Are all red men the same? No, they ain't. I've spent time in your village, talked with you, ate with you. Have I ever broken my word to any of you?"

The Utes talked among themselves for a bit. Pike understood enough Ute now to know that some of the warriors, especially Red Scar, with whom Pike had never gotten along, wanted to kill him. Others, including Blind Bull and Crazy Hawk, wanted to give Pike a chance to do what he had offered.

Finally, the warriors were quiet. "We'll trust you," Three Elk said.

Pike nodded, then pointed at Red Scar. "Just keep that son of a bitch out of my way. If you want to kill me after I've avenged your people, I'll not stop you."

"It's good. Now go," Blind Bull said.

Pike mounted his horse, realizing for the first time that he was covered with blood. "Damn," he muttered as he headed for home.

CHAPTER 19

As Cullen O'Malley stepped into the dark house with a sporting girl behind him, Pike slammed him on the side of the head with a pistol. O'Malley crumbled, not out, but close enough. Before the woman could scream or run, Pike grabbed her, softly pushed her against the wall, and put a hand over her mouth. "Quiet," he ordered, then removed his hand.

"What're you gonna do?" she blubbered.

"Nothing if you listen to me. Did he pay you?"

"Not yet."

"How much were you expecting from him?"

"Five dollars."

Pike fished around in his pocket, working by feel. Coming up with a double eagle, he put it in her hand.

From its size and weight, she knew what it was. "I can't take this," she whispered, afraid to speak any louder.

"You deserve it."

"Maybe I do, but even if I did, how do I explain it when I pay off my pimp?"

Pike took the coin back and hunted in his pockets again. With the little light flickering through the still-open door, he counted out twenty dollars in greenbacks and handed it to her. When she closed her fist around it, he said, "Now go. Take a nap or go eat or something. I don't care. Pay your pimp when you're supposed to and keep the rest for yourself. Tell him everything was fine. Don't look at me, and don't tell anyone what you saw here."

"I ain't seen anything."

"Good."

"But what if they ask questions when they find out this bum is dead? I assume you didn't knock him over the head to take him to the ball."

"No need for you to lie. He was fine when you last saw him. He wasn't dead, just a little groggy, maybe too much to drink. Now go, and don't look back. Don't talk to anyone. You do and you'll die. Understood?"

"Yep." She didn't care what happened to O'Malley. He was just a customer and a not very likable one at that. The extra fifteen dollars, plus the buck her pimp would "pay" her, would fit nicely in the small nest egg she was building.

"Scoot!"

The woman hurried out the door and moved swiftly down the street, away from the marshal's office and the saloon where her pimp held court.

Pike watched for a moment, then nodded. He hauled O'Malley to his feet and checked him for weapons, then shoved the Colt he found into his belt and tossed the smaller backup pistol across the room. He pushed the wobbly man toward the back of the house, then out the door. Grabbing O'Malley by the back of the shirt and the seat of his pants, he managed to sling him across the saddle of the horse he had taken from outside the Fat Boar saloon. He had no idea whose it was and cared less. Swiftly, he tied O'Malley down, then shoved a gag in his mouth. Pike mounted his own horse and, towing O'Malley behind him, rode out of town, taking a route behind buildings to avoid Main Street. A couple of miles away, he dismounted and whacked the groaning O'Malley over the head again, then mounted and rode on.

** ** ** ** **

When Cullen O'Malley regained his senses, he found himself tied to a tree, ropes circling his chest and another around his neck, holding him upright. His outstretched arms were tied at the wrists to small, slender trees on either side.

"Good morning, Mr. O'Malley," Pike said, not at all pleasantly.

"Who the hell are you? And what am I doing here bound up like this?" O'Malley blustered. "Where the hell are we, anyway?"

"I'm Brodie Pike. You might not have known that when you and a couple other fellas followed me a while back and I had to send you packin'. As to where you are, you are in a peaceful place in the forest where we won't be disturbed while we have a nice, short discussion. Or a long, painful one on your part. Choice is yours."

O'Malley blanched at the words. "Discussing what?" he asked, growing worried.

"You're gonna tell me who the members of the gang of devils ridin' around causin' all forms of evil are."

"I have no idea what you're talking about," O'Malley said, trying to look unconcerned and in control.

"You're not only a disgraceful son of a bitch, you're also a poor liar." He pulled out O'Malley's revolver and looked it over, to the man's dismay. "Nice piece you got here. Should have taken better care of it, but still a nice weapon. Fancy yourself a gunman, do you?"

"Damn right," O'Malley said, trying to brazen it out. You untie me and give me back that pistol, and I'll show you just how good I am."

"Alas, Mr. O'Malley, you won't be needing it much longer."

"You're gonna kill me?" O'Malley asked through gritted teeth.

"I'm not going to kill you." O'Malley showed a moment of relief that vanished fast when Pike added, "But if you don't answer my questions, it will go hard on you. Now, who're the members of that horde of dung-swillin' fiends?"

"I got no idea. I don't even know if there is anything like that in these parts." He was sweating, and his voice quavered.

"Oh, come now, Mr. O'Malley," Pike said in a calm, reasoned voice that had more than a hint of steel to it. "That's a large, steaming pile of horse manure. One more chance."

"I can't tell you what I don't know."

"Here's a reason you won't be needing this anymore," he said, tossing the pistol down. He pulled the wicked-looking pig-sticker from the sheath on his hip and stepped closer. With a sudden movement of the blade, Pike chopped off O'Malley's right thumb.

The outlaw screamed and would have fallen if not for the ropes holding him up. He clenched his teeth once more, and his face was ghostly white.

"Be damned hard to thumb back a hammer with no thumb, don't you think, boy?" Pike's voice had turned hard and cold. "Trigger finger is next, then the other thumb if you continue to be reticent about talking to me." He wiped the blade on O'Malley's shirt and re-sheathed it. "So, what's it gonna be, Mr. Gunman? Or should I say, Mr. Ex-Gunman?"

"All right, dammit, I'll talk," O'Malley gasped through the pain and fear.

"Quite reasonable of you." Pike left and got a pencil and a notepad from his saddlebags.

"So, tell me about this bunch of vigilantes."

"Not vigilantes, a safety committee. Group of fellas got together to make sure there was safety in these parts."

"Safety for who? And from who?"

"For the people of Skeeter Creek and the surrounding mines. From the Indians."

"When's the last time Indians attacked Skeeter Creek? Or the mines?"

"Don't know."

"Never would be when, I would guess. So, how many in this group of devils?"

"Twelve of 'em."

"Them? I find it hard to believe you're not one of them."

"Twelve of us," O'Malley conceded. "Plus Judge Babcock."

"So, it's like a judge and jury, eh?"

"Yes. Made it legal-like should anyone raise a stink."

"Not in any real lawman's book. And if it was a safety committee rather than a vigilance committee, why would they need legal protection, as false as it would be?"

O'Malley shrugged as best he could while being tied.

"Who else besides cranky old Josephus?"

"That the judge's first name?" O'Malley asked in surprise. "Never heard him called anything but Judge Babcock."

Pike jotted it down. "Who else?"

"Harry Peabody, Paddy Halloran, Dolph Baumann..."

"Don't know Baumann. Who's he?"

"Butcher."

"Seems appropriate, considering what you scum have been up to."

"Tate Abercrombie ..."

"The undertaker?"

"Yep." O'Malley offered up a wan smile.

"Reckon he'll need his own services soon, though he won't be able to provide them."

O'Malley gulped. "Ford Ferguson, Alf Crabtree, Les Kershaw, Ned Arnold." He stopped, face twisted in thought. "Silas Riggs, Win Gannon, and Ken Beale. That's all, I think."

Pike counted the names he had written on the list and nodded. "Lovely bunch. A judge, an undertaker, a butcher, two bankers, three bartenders, a lawyer, a shop owner, a would-be gunman, and two I don't know, now that I know about Baumann."

"Reckon that'd be Beale and Kershaw. Kershaw's a mason, Beale is a horse wrangler."

"The marshal isn't one of 'em?"

"No. Judge Babcock wanted to keep him out of it. Ain't sure why; I guess because he's an incompetent fool."

"That ain't hard to believe. Now, which of them is most responsible for the attack on the Ute village?"

"What attack on ..."

Pike dropped the pad and pencil. Yanking out his knife again, he swiftly sliced off O'Malley's right index finger, eliciting another scream. "Which ones, dammit?"

"I ain't sure of all of 'em," he said, hastily adding, "For sure, I know Halloran, Abercrombie, Crabtree, Peabody, and Gannon were there. Judge Babcock ordered it. I think Beale and Baumann were also there."

"And you?"

"I ... I ... Well, yes," he admitted in defeat and resignation, "I was there."

"Thought you said you weren't sure of all of 'em. If you were there, you'd know 'em all."

"I was havin' trouble rememberin' everyone who was there."

"It's only been a week," Pike snapped. Then, "You one of the depraved scum who raped the young girl?"

"No," O'Malley said adamantly, stiffening his back. "I think of myself as a gunman, a bringer of justice, an Indian fighter ..."

"Not much Indian fighting when it's a small village of mostly women and children." Pike's voice was tight with anger.

"Reckon you're right. You might not think much of me, but I ain't a child raper."

"Didn't do anything to stop the others from doing it, did you?"

O'Malley sagged against the ropes. "No," he whispered. "I should have. Even felt some sorry at times that I didn't. But feeling sorry for it don't make it any better, I know." He shrugged weakly.

"A little late for repenting," Pike said harshly. "But I reckon it shows a spark of humanity after all, although a mighty goddamn weak one. Might even win you a small smile from the Almighty, but I wouldn't count on it if I were you. Who was the first to abuse that poor girl?"

"Win Gannon."

Pike tore off the sheet of paper with the names of it and stuffed it into his shirt pocket. He put the notepad and the pencil back in his saddlebag, then picked up O'Malley's Colt and added it to the bag. He began saddling and bridling his horse, then did the same with the stolen horse.

O'Malley watched with a combination of fear

and hope.

Finally, Pike mounted, then touched the brim of his hat. "Good day to you, Mr. O'Malley. May the Lord have mercy on whatever soul you might have left. No decent person will." He picked up the reins of the stolen horse and began to ride slowly out of the glade.

"Hey! Pike!" O'Malley yelled.

Pike looked over his shoulder. "Yes?"

"You said you weren't gonna kill me!"

"I'll keep my word. I'm not gonna kill you."

"You leave me out here like this and I'll die just the same, you son of a bitch."

Pike smiled grimly. "Never said I wouldn't leave you to die. Just said I wouldn't kill you. So long." He rode out, the imprecations screamed at him by Cullen O'Malley falling on deaf ears.

CHAPTER 20

Pike knew he couldn't take on all six of the remaining actual perpetrators, though one had been taken care of already. He didn't mind dying—indeed, he would almost welcome it—but he wanted all thirteen of them to pay in full for their wickedness. Dying afterward would mean little to him.

So, he figured he would lessen the odds a little at a time, taking on one or two of the evildoers as he had in Arrowhead. O'Malley had been the first. He rode to the large cave on the hidden road, where he had laid in supplies and gear two days ago. There he unwrapped the .52-caliber Sharps he had used as a sniper in the Civil War from its protective covering of buffalo hide and canvas. He broke it down and cleaned it carefully, then pieced it back together. He grabbed a bandolier of shells for the weapon and slung it over his shoulder.

It was still light out, and he decided a meal would be a good thing before leaving on his mission, although he had no desire for food. His only hunger was for revenge, but to get that, he would have to keep his body fueled, so he ate a deer shank left over from the day before and washed it down with fresh, cold water from the spring that trickled down the wall of the cave near the back, as well as two small swallows from a bottle of whiskey, but no more. Finally, he burped, cleaned his hands on a rag, and stood. "It's time," he muttered.

He saddled his horse, kicked dirt over the fire, and slid the rifle into the special scabbard on the saddle that would protect it. Dusk settled over the pines and firs as he rode toward Skeeter Creek. It was full dark when he reached the town, and once again, he skirted the buildings, keeping to the back streets and alleys. He stopped and led his horse into a decrepit barn where it was likely that no one would bother her. He slung two canteens of water over his shoulders and shoved a pouch with the last bits of cooked meat and some jerky into a coat pocket. Taking the rifle, still in the scabbard, off the saddle, he strode fifty yards away. He tied a rope securely around the scabbard, and with the other end of the rope in his teeth, he deftly climbed a tree, then gingerly crept along a large branch until he was standing on the roof of the tobacconist's shop. The owner would not be on the job until well into the morning. He carefully hauled the rifle up and moved across the roof, then sat and waited.

As the sun began to peek above the mountains, Pike slid the rifle out of the scabbard and scooted forward until he was on the edge of the roof overlooking Main Street. He had a good view of many of the buildings where his targets would be at some time of the morning. He slid a shell into the Sharps and waited some more.

It was more than an hour before Alf Crabtree and Win Gannon came out of Sontag's restaurant and stopped to talk on the sidewalk. Pike grinned grimly as he sighted through the long copper scope. Crabtree turned to face Gannon, whose back was to the restaurant door, and Pike fired. The big Sharps bullet caught Crabtree just above the back of the right knee, shattering the patella on its downward trajectory on the way out. He collapsed with a shriek of agony. Shocked, Gannon froze for a moment. Pike ejected the spent shell and slid a new one home. As Gannon moved to kneel at Crabtree's side, Pike fired again. The bullet tore Gannon's shoulder apart, almost separating it from his body. Screaming, he fell half atop his friend. Most folks ran for cover, though three men knelt by the wounded pair. They cast their eyes about, searching for the source of the gunfire, but saw nothing. The wind had whisked away the gun's smoke within seconds of the shots being fired.

Pike slithered back from the edge of the roof and sat up, the rifle across his lap. He wanted the two men to suffer, so he had aimed to hurt them, not kill them. Death would visit them later.

The sun in the bright, cloudless sky was warm, though winter would not be long in coming. He took a couple of sips of water, trying to keep his mind blank. He was pleased with what he had just done, but he was filled with self-recrimination at the knowledge that he would be responsible for what he now had to do.

It was always thus, he knew, unable to keep the grim thoughts at bay. Always, he had tried to be the good guy. To help others who had been oppressed or set upon. Too often, his efforts led to heartbreak and trouble.

He could see none of the good he had done, only the bad. If he was still alive when this was over, he decided he would go to an even more remote place, one higher in the San Juan Mountains, perhaps, where no one would ever find him. A place far from people, both white and red. There would be no one to bother him, no one to ask for his help, and no one whom he thought needed his help. He could live out the rest of his days as a hermit in quiet solitude and let his soul rot in its own misery.

He shook his head after a while, having a little more success at flinging away the rancid thoughts. He almost smiled. There would be no need for such a life, he figured. He likely would be dead before the month was out, and that would be to the benefit of everyone except the wretched bastards who had perpetrated this latest abomination against the Utes. Of course, there was always the possibility—no, the likelihood—that his friendship with the Utes would not keep them from killing him if he survived this vendetta. That would be fitting, he decided. It wouldn't matter either way.

Despite all the thinking and soul-searching, Pike had kept an ear on the sounds below. It took a while for the tumult to die down and the wounded to be taken by the town's only doctor to be tended. With the shouting, he did not hear Judge Babcock order a search. He became aware of it only when he heard someone climbing the tree he had used to reach the roof.

"Damn," he muttered. He swiftly untied the rope from the scabbard, slid the rifle in, and set it aside. He quickly made a lasso and moved toward the rear edge of the roof, slightly to the side of where the tree was, planning to hang the newcomer. He stretched out on his belly and peered carefully over the edge.

He swore again. The man shinnying up the tree was not one of the men he was hunting. Pike really didn't want to kill a man who had not been involved in the Indians' violation, even if he wasn't without sin, but he could not allow himself to be discovered, not with the town up in arms. He slithered over and stretched out on his back, knees bent, boot soles flat on the roof, inches from the end. He raised his head and watched. A few moments later, the searcher's head popped up. Pike's legs shot out, and his boot heels caught the man in the forehead. He fell and crashed down through the branches of the tree, giving only one yelp of surprise and pain.

Pike knew he had kicked the man too hard, and the crashing did not bode well for the man's health.

Working fast, Pike tied the scabbard again and lowered the rifle carefully, then he scrambled down the old oak. The man lay awkwardly on the ground. He was alive, but his neck appeared to be broken. Pike figured he was also concussed and had other broken bones, which together would prove fatal sooner rather than later. He shook his head. "Fouled up again, Brodie," he muttered. But it couldn't be undone, and he had to get away.

He grabbed the man's shirt, dragged him into a cluster of bushes, and dropped him there. Then he hurried to grab the sniper rifle and rushed to the barn. Quickly but carefully, he strapped the scabbard to the saddle, tightened the cinch, and cautiously rode out. He headed away from town behind the barn, hoping the structure, the scattering of trees, and the sunlight shining on Skeeter Creek would keep him from being seen.

The mountains shot up high and fast about a mile and a half west of town. The townsfolk rarely went that way, seeing nothing but a wall of rock in their way. Pike had explored the area in the past several weeks and had found a way through, a crevice barely wide enough for him and his horse. It was hidden behind a fairly tight stand of lodgepole pines interspersed with aspens. Wax currants and chokecherry bushes grew in profusion among the trees.

The narrow rock passage wriggled like a drunken snake for more than half a mile before emptying into a small meadow less than fifty yards in circumference. A thin trail wove upward through more pines and aspens into the mountains to the northwest. The trees grew sparse, but then the land leveled out for a mile or so. Eventually, Pike passed through another crevice, this one larger, and followed the trail down.

Coming to another flat, he stopped amid the pines and firs and prepared to settle in for the rest of the afternoon and the night. This was the last even mildly reasonable place to stop before the trail ran its treacherous course down the mountain and wove through areas where there were steep drop-offs on one side and tall, harsh cliffs on the other. Pike had no desire to chance that trek at night. He had tried it once and come out alive only through luck and a horse with a good sense of danger. It was a miserable camp, though he had a small fire. He had no food or coffee, and even if he had, there was nothing to prepare them.

He was off again at first light, tired, hungry, and irritated, mostly at himself. He fumed for several miles before spitting his self-anger into the dirt. "Lord, if you're really up there watching over things," he muttered, "all I ask is that I finish this with no more troubles, and then I disappear." Somehow, he doubted his plea would be answered.

Early in the afternoon, he reached his cabin. He stayed behind some trees, dismounted, and waited, watching. He was certain the men from Skeeter Creek had no idea where the cabin was, but the Utes did, and they could be waiting for him, still enraged at the horrific events he had brought to Fallen Timber's people. After an hour, leaving the horse tied to a maple, he strode forward, still cautious.

The cabin door was unlatched, making him all the more vigilant. He pulled out a Colt and held it upright, muzzle to the sky, thumb on the hammer. With the toe of his right boot, he gently pushed the door open and waited. He heard nothing, but that didn't mean no one was there. He sniffed warily.

Since he had not used the cabin for a while, he thought he might be able to smell someone if a person was lurking inside. That, too, proved fruitless.

With an inward sigh, he kicked the door fully open and shoved inside very quickly, cocking his revolver as he did. He crouched, ready for an enemy. But there was no one. No friends, either. Taking a deep breath of relief, he uncocked his pistol and put it away. Despite it still being daylight, he lit a couple of lanterns, and the single-room cabin took on a cheerier air.

He took a quick look around the room, but nothing appeared to have been disturbed. He was certain he had latched the door when he left, so he figured one of the Utes, probably Crazy Hawk, had been there.

He went out and got his horse and put her in the small log corral, then unsaddled and tended her. The mule was still as he had left it, with a good supply of forage. The animal brayed, either in greeting or annoyance at not having been left enough feed. Pike did not know which and cared little. He took his saddle, saddlebags, and scabbard into the cabin and dropped the former two on the floor in a corner and the latter gently on the table.

He latched the door and shoved the table against it. It wouldn't stop anyone who was determined to get in, but it would give him a few moments to get ready to defend himself.

He started a fire in the stove, keeping it small. He wanted to cook a meal but did not want to attract attention. As small a fire as this was, the smoke coming out of the stovepipe would not be seen unless someone was within a few yards of the place. He cut off a hunk of salted elk that had been wrapped in buckskin and slapped it in a pan with a little fat, then ground some coffee beans and dumped them in a pot. He sniffed the bucket of water in the corner; it smelled all right to him, and he figured if he let the coffee boil, it would kill anything harmful. He set the pot on the stove.

After eating, Pike cleaned the Sharps, then crawled into his buffalo-robe bed and was asleep instantly.

CHAPTER 21

Pike waited in the dark, leaning against the corner of a building deep in the shadows. It had been three days since he shot Gannon and Crabtree. He had spent one night at the cabin, then rode hard for Skeeter Creek, making it in three days instead of the usual four. He knew where his two wounded victims were since there was only one doctor. He was certain the men hadn't been taken home, but he needed to know the routines of the others.

On this night, he had left his horse a mile away in a cluster of cottonwoods and aspens and walked to Skeeter Creek. His first stop was the doctor's office. It was locked, but Pike had no trouble breaking in, though it was a bit noisy.

"That you, Doc?" a weak voice called from an inner room.

Pike headed that way. Again, the voice called out.

"No, I'm not the doctor," Pike said as he walked into the room. The curtains were closed, so Pike lit a coal-oil lamp, keeping the flame low. "I'm the man who's here to finish your execution. Shootin' you was just the beginnin'.'"

He walked to the side of the bed, and in the lantern light, he looked down at Win Gannon, one of the town's bankers. He held the light up so Gannon could see his face.

"Who're you?" Gannon asked, confused. "Do I know you?"

"Likely you don't know me, but our acquaintance will be brief. I just wanted you to see the man who is avengin' the deaths of a band of innocent Utes."

"I don't know what you're talking about."

"You know quite well what I'm talkin' about, Mr. Gannon." The frigid wind of a mountain winter was but a warm summer breeze compared to the iciness of Pike's eyes and voice. "One might think a man who had the stones to lead the way in raping an eleven-year-old girl would have the stones to own up to it. But I reckon I was expectin' too much."

"What are you ...?"

"If you know any prayers, you best say 'em." He set the lamp on a nearby table and found some cloth, which he wadded up and shoved into Gannon's mouth. "You caused that innocent little girl very much pain," Pike said as rage boiled up inside of him at the memory of Winter Sky. He pulled his knife. "You'll never suffer as much as that child did, but you will suffer."

Pike pulled back the blanket exposing Gannon's chest. Holding down Gannon's good arm with one hand, Pike ran the tip of the blade from the man's clavicle down to his hip, but not too deep. Gannon's eyes bugged, and he feebly tried to free his arm.

Pike made the same cut a few inches to the left. Then another, and one more. Blood ran from each down his side to create small pools. "Feelin' good?" Pike asked in a harsh voice. "Let's see if we can make you feel even better." He eased the knife several inches into the left side of Gannon's abdomen, then tugged it across his body, slicing through muscle and intestines. Every inch he moved the blade gave Pike another image of Winter Sky's agony. He had to resist plunging the knife into Gannon's heart. That would not make him suffer enough.

Finally, Pike lifted the blade free and wiped it on the blanket. "I ain't sure, Mr. Gannon, but I've heard such a wound will kill you, though it could take a while. You might use the time to ruminate on your wickedness."

Pike walked into the next room, where Alf Crabtree lay. He had been calling out all along, but Pike had ignored him.

"Who're you?" Crabtree asked, his voice quaking. "What'd you do to Win?"

"Gave him a small dose of the sufferin' he and you gave Winter Sky."

"Who?"

"That little Ute girl you and Gannon and those others abused in the most painful and shameful way. His anger had not dimmed one iota.

"An Indian girl? You're concerned about an Indian girl?" Crabtree was surprised but also worried.

"Don't matter much whether she was Indian or white. She was eleven years old and never hurt no one in her short life, but degenerates like you and Gannon thought it'd be fun to abuse her most sinfully. Now it's time to pay."

"What ... What're you gonna do?

"Make certain you never do that again to anyone. I could remove certain parts of you to ensure that, but I ain't an animal like you." He latched onto Crabtree's throat and squeezed, letting the rage inside him flow through his arms and hands as he slowly pressed the life out of Crabtree. The man fought, but he was too weak to do anything.

Pike finally unlocked his hands. He was breathing heavily, not from exertion but from the emotions still seething through him. Finally taking a deep, calming breath, he left the doctor's office and headed to Dolph Baumann's butcher shop. He kept to the shadows, though there was no one on the streets. He had little trouble getting inside this place either through the back door. He picked up a blood-crusted cleaver, then waited in a corner of the main room.

It was still well before dawn when Baumann arrived at his shop, unlocking the front door with his key. He fired up a lantern, then reached for the cleaver he always left stuck in the wood of his butcher's block. He was surprised when it was not there and scratched his head in puzzlement.

Pike stepped out of the dark corner and said softly, "Lookin' for this?" When the German butcher turned, Pike whipped the cleaver down on Baumann's head, splitting it from crown nearly to chin.

Baumann went down, dead before he could utter a sound.

Pike wiped his hands on an apron he found near the counter, then dropped it atop Baumann. He slipped out the back and unhurriedly headed across the field to where his horse was tethered a few yards into the forest. He tightened the cinch, stripped off the hobbles, mounted, and rode out.

"Three more down," he muttered. "A good night's work." There were still nine to go. He took a circuitous route in case he was followed, however unlikely that was, and ended up in the meadow where he had saved Fallen Timber and Light Elk. He had stashed some food and water there, and he set up a camp. He stayed there for two nights. On the third evening, as dusk was creeping over the mountains, he headed back to Skeeter Creek. He left his horse in the empty ramshackle barn he had used the night he had shot Gannon and Crabtree.

He walked to Paddy Halloran's house and waited. Halloran was one of the bartenders in town, and he was among those who had attacked the village. It began to rain, something Pike had expected and had planned for by wearing his slicker. About midnight, Halloran left the Dirty Water saloon and headed home. As he neared his house, Pike called from the shadows, "Hey, Paddy."

The Irishman turned. "Who's there?" he asked, not concerned.

"Got some information for you."

"No information'll interest me."

"This will. Made me a fresh strike up the mountain a ways. I need a partner, and I heard you needed some extra money. Thought you might like to join up with me."

Intrigued, Halloran walked to the corner of the house, where he promptly caught a pistol barrel across the forehead. He staggered, but Pike caught him before he fell and dragged him around to the back, where he dropped him. Pike tied the bartender's hands and ankles with rawhide strips and waited.

Halloran awoke before long and realized he was bound. "What the hell?" he mumbled as he tried to free himself.

Pike walked into Halloran's field of vision. "Howdy."

"Who the devil are you?" the man demanded.

"No devil, Mr. Halloran. I'm an angel. An avenging angel here to make you pay for attacking a village of peaceable Utes and for abusing a child in the most wicked fashion." He stepped up and jammed a boot on the back of Halloran's neck, then pushed the bartender's face into the mud and the inch-deep water.

Halloran bucked and struggled to no avail, and before long, he was dead.

As with the others, Pike did not care that any of those he had killed might be family men. That some women and children had to suffer the loss of these men was nothing compared with the wanton slaughter of a village of Indians and the gruesome debasement of a child. If they knew what their husbands and fathers had done, they would loathe those men, or they would if they were true Christian women and children.

He left and got his horse, then headed toward the small wooded hill that rose a hundred yards from the back of the last building in Skeeter Creek. He rode along the tree line for a bit, then pulled a few yards into the forest. Once more, he waited.

He would be taking a chance by staying here for as long as he was planning to, but he thought it was worth it. A few hours later, the rain stopped, for which he was grateful. Just after dawn broke, hazy and cool, Pike saw the man he had identified as Ken Beale moving toward the corral at the far end of the town. When he reached it, he climbed over the logs and wandered among the dozen or so horses.

Pike guessed that most if not all the horses were mustangs, at least partially broken if Beale was moving about so easily in their midst. He was, after all, a bronc buster.

Pike drew the sniper rifle from its scabbard. Resting his shoulder against a ponderosa pine, Pike took aim and fired. The bullet hit one of the corral's upright posts, which was where he had planned to put it. Hurriedly he reloaded and drew a bead again.

Beale turned to find out where the shot had come from.

Pike fired again and gave a small smile of satisfaction when the bullet shattered Beale's right hip, dropping him to the ground. The bronc buster's scream spooked the horses, who began shuffling nervously and stamping their hooves.

Pike fired one more time, hitting a metal pail near the back of the corral. The bullet sent the thing skittering with a dull clang, which was enough to turn the herd into a seething, bucking mass of hooves seeking an escape. There was none unavailable.

Beale tried to drag himself toward the side of the corral, where he might be able to roll under the lowest log, but a hoof caught him on the head. He slumped with another scream, which did nothing to calm the animals. Soon he was being pounded into the mud as the horses grew even wilder.

Pike waited until he was sure Beale was dead or would be soon. He carefully put the sniper rifle back in the scabbard and rode off, keeping to the trees until he was far enough away that he could use the road. He took his hidden road and pushed on until he got the big cave he had been using as a sanctuary lately. Although he was exhausted, he took care of his horse, then managed to heat up a little food. After that and a cup of coffee, he stretched out on the bedroll he kept there. He was asleep almost as soon as he laid down.

In the morning, he felt almost human again. After eating, he took stock and realized he needed more supplies, and he wanted to spend a night or two at his house. However ramshackle it was, it was his home. He kicked out the fire, mounted his horse, and rode out.

CHAPTER 22

Pike was half a dozen miles from home when the arrow caught him high in the back on the left side. He almost fell off his horse but managed to hang on. A second arrow flashed past a moment later, then a third, which skimmed the horse's flank. The animal bolted across the meadow. After a minute or so, Pike was able to bring the horse back to a trot, and he looked behind him. The Indian was coming on quickly, bow nocked and ready, so Pike pulled a Colt and fired twice. He didn't hit anything, but it sent the warrior racing toward the trees.

Pike slipped the revolver back into the holster. Slumped over, almost lying on the horse's neck, he rode on. He was dizzy and filled with pain when the horse stopped in front of the house of her own accord. Pike tried to slide off the horse but fell. He lay there for a while—he had no idea how long—before he got wobblily to his feet and staggered into the house. Once inside, he collapsed on the bed of buffalo robes on his left side. He looked down and saw that the arrowhead had come almost all the way through. Without a thought to what he was doing, he tried to roll onto his back and snapped the shaft of the arrow off. He groaned and passed out.

** ** ** ** **

Crazy Hawk approached Pike's house warily. He was surprised to see his friend's horse wandering loose, still saddled. That was highly unusual for Pike. He dismounted and called, "Brodie." When there was no response, he called again. When there was still no response, he cautiously pushed on the door, which was partially opened. "Brodie," he called again, then he saw the lump lying on its side on the robes, back toward him.

The Ute hurried across the few feet, seeing the arrow as soon as he took his first step. He let loose with soft curses in his language, followed by a few in English. He rolled Pike just a bit toward him, eliciting a deep groan. The arrowhead had come through almost its full length.

Crazy Hawk rocked back on his heels. He could grab the arrowhead and jerk it free, but he wasn't sure Pike would survive it or the blood loss. He wished he knew something about herbs and roots and other things the People used for various ailments and injuries, but all that was handled by the women and medicine men. Even if he did know about them, there were none to be had in the cabin or anywhere near here that he knew of.

He realized he could not leave Pike here like this long enough for him to get help. Without removing the arrow, the wound might get infected. He made a decision and found an old shirt of Pike's. Kneeling next to his friend, he grabbed the arrowhead in strong fingers and yanked. Even though Pike was unconscious, he hissed in pain. Crazy Hawk slapped the shirt against the bleeding wound and used the sleeves to tie in place. It wasn't perfect, but it would have to do. He laid Pike on his back.

"Hang on, my friend," he muttered, then headed outside. Though time was of the essence, he took the time to unsaddle Pike's horse, put her in the corral with the mule, and made sure they had hay and water. He carried the saddle with Pike's Winchester and special rifle inside and placed them in a corner. Then he was on his pony and riding hard.

It took him only four hours to make the trip to his village that usually took six or more. When he arrived, his horse was nearly played out. He charged into Blind Bull's lodge, and without any preliminaries or politeness, ordered Little Raven to gather whatever medicines she needed and get ready to ride. He charged out but was back in ten minutes with two saddled ponies.

Blind Bull came out of the lodge with Little Raven. "What is this?" he demanded.

"Brodie is wounded bad. Needs help. Come, Little Raven, we go."

Blind Bull helped his daughter onto her pony, and she and Crazy Hawk raced out of the village. He stood there watching them for a minute, then turned and headed to the horse herd. He saddled one, gathered four more, and rode out soon after, herding the four extra horses ahead of him but not pushing. He didn't waste time, but he was not in a headlong rush.

It was dark when Crazy Hawk and Little Raven arrived at the cabin. The warrior went to tend the horses.

The woman ran into the house, lighted a lamp, and went to Pike's side. She tried to keep her emotions in check as she looked at her man, for that was what she considered him. She quickly started a fire in the stove and grabbed a pot, then laid out her herbs, and within minutes, she was cooking up a poultice.

As she was applying it to Pike's wound front and back, Crazy Hawk entered. He knew better than to ask how Pike was going, but he knelt beside his sister and picked up the two pieces of the arrow. Anger ripped through him when he looked at the markings. He wanted to head back to the village immediately and even started to rise.

Little Raven, just who was finishing applying the poultice, stopped him. "Where are you going?" she asked.

"Back to the village."

"You know who did this?"

"Yes."

"He won't go anywhere. Wait. It's dark, and you've traveled much today. Tomorrow you will hunt and leave me and Brodie food, then go back."

Crazy Hawk growled in annoyance but nodded.

Several hours later, Little Raven was asleep. Crazy Hawk was dozing but the sound of horses approaching brought him fully awake. He made sure he had the pistol he had started carrying recently and quickly prepared his bow. He slipped outside, making himself a target only for the couple of seconds when he opened the door.

"Is this how you greet your father?" Blind Bull asked as he dismounted.

"Welcome," Crazy Hawk said. "Why're you here?"

"Brought food and extra horses if we need them."

"Toy-ack—Thank you."

They took care of the horses but had to hobble the four extra ones since there was no room in the small corral. As they worked, Blind Bull asked, "How is our friend?"

"Bad."

"What happened?"

"Shot with an arrow."

"An arrow? Not many white-eyes use a bow."

"None as far as I know."

"So, it must have been one of our people."

"Red Scar.

"You're sure?"

"Come, I'll show you."

The two men went into the house, where Crazy Hawk showed his father the arrow.

Blind Bull nodded. "I'll make him one whose name is not spoken."

"No, I'll kill him."

"You are needed here with your white friend."

Crazy Hawk argued vehemently, finally saying, "Brodie will want to kill him."

"No. Red Scar is one of the People, and we must do this among ourselves."

"Brodie won't be happy."

"He is killing his own kind for what they did to the People. It's only right that the People do the same."

Crazy Hawk nodded. "Sleep first."

With a yawn, Blind Bull got his blanket off his horse and laid it out in a corner. He was asleep in moments.

** ** ** ** **

It took Pike a little while to realize where he was and a little longer to remember why. He opened his eyes to see Little Raven sitting by his side, smiling.

"About time you wake," she said.

"How long was I out?"

"At least two days. Don't know how long before Crazy Hawk and I got here." She told him how she and Crazy Hawk came to be here.

"Where is he?"

"Carin' for the ponies. How you feelin'?"

"I've felt better, I can tell you. But not so bad, I reckon. I expect you had something to do with that."

"Just used poultice on wounds and changed it many times."

"Well, I am obliged, Raven."

The Ute woman's already dark skin deepened in embarrassment. She helped him sit up and lean against the wall.

Crazy Hawk walked in and asked, "Is he ...?" He stopped and grinned. "You look damned good for a white-eye with two holes in his shoulder."

"Thanks," Pike said, failing to keep the sarcasm

out of his voice. "Raven tells me you went through a lot to help me."

"A lot more than you would've done for me." Crazy Hawk smiled.

"Probably right," Pike replied, smiling weakly. "Since I don't see the arrow, I figure you took it. I reckon you know who did this."

Crazy Hawk nodded.

"You gonna tell me?"

"Red Scar."

"Well, when you get back to your village, you best tell that son of a bitch that his time on this earth is mighty short. Soon's I get well enough to ride, I'll see to it that he pays."

"No."

"You aimin' to stop me?"

"Nope." When Pike gave him a quizzical look, he added, "His time ain't short. His time is over."

"What's that mean?"

"Blind Bull killed him."

Pike grew angry but then relaxed. He nodded. After a moment of silence, he asked, "Why'd you come here when you found me, Hawk?"

"Came to steal your mule." The Ute burst out laughing. "I been here a few times to check on that damned beast since you went off and left him here. I let him loose the first time, but he stayed around. I always knew mules were stubborn, but I hadn't realized they were stupid, too. Give the animal his freedom, and he hangs around here waitin' for you."

"Does seem foolish. You headin' back to the village soon?"

"Once I know you're all right."

"I'll be fine."

"I stay," Little Raven said. "You go."

Crazy Hawk thought that over, then nodded. "I'll go huntin' and bring in some meat for you both, then I'll go. But first, what about the white-eyes who ...?"

"Five of the ones who made the attack are dead," Pike said flatly. "There's two others, and four who weren't in on the attack but were with the others in what they called a safety commission. Soon's I'm well enough to ride, I'll get the two worst ones first, then the others."

"Good."

** ** ** ** **

After three weeks, Pike was getting itchy, and he decided it was time to finish his mission. His rage had not disappeared, though it had lessened to a simmer as he recuperated. It began to build again as he prepared to leave.

"Time for you to go home, Raven," he said one morning.

She nodded and began packing her things while Pike saddled their horses. Late that afternoon, they rode into Many Snows' village. He spent the night in a lodge with Little Raven, and he set out in the morning for Skeeter Creek.

CHAPTER 23

Pike knocked on Tate Abercrombie's front door. He waited for a bit, then did so again. When there was still no response, he pounded on the door.

The undertaker's voice came from just inside the door. "What the hell do you want? It's after midnight."

"What the hell do you think I want at an undertaker's? I got some business for you."

"Can't it wait 'til morning? You woke me up, and I'm not in the right frame of mind to conduct business at this hour."

"Reckon it could wait."

"Good."

"I'll just leave the corpse here leanin' on your door. You'll not be able to miss him in the mornin'."

"All right, dammit, all right." After a moment, he opened the door and found the point of a large knife touching him just under his chin.

"Back up, Mr. Abercrombie." When he did, Pike kicked the door shut with his bootheel. "You have any coffins?"

"Well, yes, of course." Abercrombie tried to assess how crazy this man was. "Couple of good ones in the back room. A few cheap ones out back."

"Let's go take a look at the good ones." He removed the knife from under the man's chin, turned the tall, angular undertaker around, and shoved him forward. The lantern Abercrombie was still carrying provided enough light for Pike's needs.

Abercrombie, still clad in his nightclothes, took a few steps, then hesitated. Pike kicked him behind the left knee, and the undertaker fell to his knees, almost dropping the lantern. "Get up and get movin'."

"I can't get up now that you've kicked me."

"I believe you can." Pike pushed the blade into the back of Abercrombie's neck.

Abercrombie scrambled to his feet and marched on. He stopped just inside the back room, where two fancy silk-lined coffins sat on sawhorses.

"Put the lantern on that table." When Abercrombie did so, Pike asked, "Which one do you like best?"

"What?"

"You prefer the one with red silk or white?"

"What?" Abercrombie asked again.

"It's a simple question."

"The red, I guess," Abercrombie said nervously.

Pike nodded, then tossed a rope loop over Abercrombie's shoulders and yanked it tight when it was halfway down his arms.

"What the ...?"

Pike shoved his dirty bandanna into Abercrombie's mouth, then wound the rope around the undertaker down to his ankles, where he tied it snuggly. Despite his recent wound, Pike had little trouble lifting the thin undertaker into the red-silk-lined coffin.

"There is a price to be paid," Pike said through lips tight with anger, "when someone commits an unspeakable act." He grinned grimly down at Abercrombie. "An eleven-year-old girl is not a plaything for a gang of degenerate men's sick amusement. She was not just abused, she was tortured. Alas, I cannot make you suffer nearly as much as she did at your hands and the hands of the others, but I can make damn sure you will have an eternity to deliberate on your wickedness with your pals when you get to hell. And hell is surely where you're goin', Mr. Abercrombie."

He shoved aside the lower part of Abercrombie's nightwear, then stabbed him deep in each thigh and twisted the knife a few times. The heavy flow of blood told him he had nicked the large artery in each.

"In the little time you have left, you can repent or at least pray. Goodbye, Mr. Abercrombie." He wiped his knife clean on Abercrombie's nightshirt, then closed the coffin's lid and locked it. He took a few minutes to regain control of himself, then left, first checking that no one was nearby.

There was time for another visit, but he decided he was not prepared for it. He rode out, taking the back trail for a few miles, where he made a little camp. For the next two nights, he watched his new victim from the shadows, learning his habits. Given the way the man held himself, Pike figured he was the one who had been wounded in the attack. From the few people about and his victim, he got the feeling the town was on edge, and he wanted to think he was the cause. A number of prominent citizens had been killed in gruesome ways. Even though there had been no trouble for almost a month until Abercrombie had been dealt with, he sensed tenseness in the air.

On the second night, while his victim was occupied in a saloon as was usual, he went to Silas Peabody's small house, which was next door to his mercantile store. He lived alone.

He circled behind the house and stopped at the front corner in the shadows. Since there was no rear door, the front would have to do. With a swift look around, he determined no one was there to see him, and he swiftly slipped inside through the unlocked door. He stopped and leaned back against the portal, allowing his eyes to adjust to the darkness within. He found a lamp and lit it, adjusting the flame to the bare minimum, then looked over the interior to memorize the furniture and the layout, which took no more than ten minutes. He extinguished the lamp and opened the door an inch. When he was satisfied, he moved outside swiftly and headed up the dark, virtually empty street to the back of Peabody's general store. He jimmied open the rear door and went inside, where he gathered up the few things he needed and placed them in a sack.

He slung the bag over his shoulder and walked purposefully back to the house, then leaned against a tree some yards from the back of the house and waited.

It took more than an hour, but finally, the coal-oil lamp was lit. After another fifteen minutes, it was dimmed. Just to be sure, he waited a bit longer, then strode across the distance and around to the front of the house.

Once more, he moved inside and let his eyes adjust. A dim light came from the lamp, enough to see by since he knew the layout of the two rooms in the well-kept house. He stood over the bed for a moment, watching Peabody and letting the rage build again.

Then he carefully lay his sack down, opened it, and pulled out a handkerchief and a small bottle. He poured a good amount of the liquid from the bottle on the handkerchief, keeping it at arm's length. He knelt and carefully set the bottle on the floor, laid the handkerchief over Peabody's nose and mouth, and gently held it down. Peabody barely moved. Pike did not know how long it would be before the chloroform took effect or how long it would last, but he gave it several minutes. He left the handkerchief where it was, cautiously put the cork in the bottle, and set it aside. He waited for several more minutes, then flicked Peabody's ear sharply several times but got no response.

With a grim grin, Pike took the rope out of the bag, tightly wrapped two lengths around Peabody's legs and the bed, and tied it tight, then did the same with his arms and torso. He pulled the handkerchief off Peabody's mouth and shoved it into his mouth as a gag, then sat down to wait.

It took longer than he had hoped but less time than he expected before Peabody began to stir. He snorted a few times and tried to turn over. Pike rose and walked over to the bed. "Good evening, Mr. Peabody," he said in a cold tone. "It's past time you paid for your sins. In case you're unsure of what those transgressions were, well, attackin' a village of peaceful Indians was one. Tormenting and molesting an eleven-year-old girl was even worse."

Pike took the glass chimney off the lamp, then bent and removed two sticks of dynamite from the bag. Peabody's eyes widened in fear as Pike lit the two long fuses from the low-burning wick of the lamp and tossed the dynamite under the bed. "Farewell, Mr. Peabody."

Pike swiftly headed out the door and went behind the house. He stopped several buildings away and waited in the darkness.

Moments later, Peabody's house was blown to splinters. With a nod of satisfaction, Pike strolled unhurriedly to the rickety barn he had left his horse in. Instead of keeping to the shadows this time, he crossed Main Street in the open since everyone who was up and about was rushing to the scene of the blast and the fire it had sparked.

** ** ** ** **

As he sat in his cave and relaxed over the last of the venison, he pondered his next move. He had never considered the possible ramifications of what he had done. He didn't regret it in the least, but he was becoming aware of the possibility that the townsfolk of Skeeter Creek might bring in a marshal authorized by Colorado Territory's governor. Now that he thought about it, he wondered why they had not done so after the first series of gruesome killings before Pike was wounded. It was possible that they didn't want trouble. An Indian village and an Indian girl had been brutalized, which wouldn't mean much to the authorities, but with the Territory on the brink of statehood, trouble of any kind might put a kink in that. The townsfolk and the miners would not want the interference a territorial investigation would bring.

He considered not extending his quest for vengeance to the four remaining members of the safety committee, but he realized that at least one more had to pay the price—Judge Josephus Babcock. The other three he would leave alone, but the judge who had ordered the attack on Fallen Timber's village had to pay.

He thought for a few minutes about capturing Babcock and turning him over to Blind Bull, Crazy Hawk, and the others, but he decided that would be foolish. Should word of that get out, however unlikely that was, it would bring the wrath of the Territory, and more importantly the Army, down on the Utes. Pike had already brought too much trouble to those Indians.

He finally decided Babcock would be the last. The other three had not taken part. While they might have done so if given the chance, they had not, so he decided he would leave them be.

Once he had taken care of Babcock, though, he would have to decide what to do. Remaining here might be a problem if anyone connected him to the killings around Skeeter Creek. He would hate to just leave since that would mean saying goodbye to those with whom he had become friends—Crazy Hawk and Blind Bull. Worse would be leaving Little Raven. Considering the trouble he had brought to people in his past, though, that probably would be better for her.

"Bah," he muttered. He tossed the dregs of coffee from his cup into the fire and went to his bedroll, thinking he would make that decision when he had finished his business here, but sleep was long in coming.

In the morning, he downed a tasteless breakfast and headed toward Skeeter Creek. Rather than spend another night in the smaller cave, he stayed on the hidden trail before moving onto the road leading to the town. He stopped late the next afternoon in a thick stand of aspens, the leaves of which were beginning to turn, and napped a little, rousing himself after dark. He ate a bit of jerky and drank from his canteen, then he saddled his horse and rode on. He stopped and tied the mare to a loose board on the back of the poorly-built courthouse, where he easily forced the back door open and went inside. He took a seat in the rickety chair in the small office and rested his boots on the desk. Moments later, he saw the scalps hanging on the wall, and a new blast of rage ripped through him. He rose, took them down, and wrapped them gently in the small territorial flag that hung from a stand in the corner, then went back to the desk and sat again with his feet up. He figured he had several hours before the judge arrived just before dawn as he always did. He dozed a little.

The clanking of the lock and the squeaking of the front door woke Pike. He rubbed a hand across his face and rose, gliding to stand beside the door between the courtroom and Babcock's office. There would be no killing related to the man's profession this time. No, this would be over quickly, and Pike would be on his way.

The door opened, and Babcock stepped inside. He made it two steps before Pike grabbed his hair, jerked his head back, and slid the blade of his knife across the judge's throat. The bounty hunter held the man up for a moment, then let him fall to the floor in a pool of blood.

Pike grabbed the scalps, went outside, mounted, and headed down the road, unaware that he had a tail.

CHAPTER 24

Pike stopped in front of his house three days after disposing of Judge Josephus Babcock. He had considered just riding off, heading anywhere but here, but he had some things at the cabin that would come in handy, and he could use the mule—if the animal was still there—to carry whatever supplies he needed. He had set the animal free when he last left for Skeeter Creek. It had stayed the time Crazy Hawk set him free, so maybe he had done so this time.

He was glad to see the animal grazing in the meadow not far from the cabin. He caught him and put him in the corral with his mare, then went inside the cabin and fired up the stove. He put on some coffee and threw pieces of the rabbit he had killed that morning into a frying pan. Soon he sat at his table and ate without much enthusiasm.

After he finished, he took the flag-wrapped scalps and buried them behind the cabin. He didn't know if the Utes would approve, but to him, it was a proper burial. He said a few prayers vaguely remembered from his youth, then went back into the cabin and sat at the table.

Now that he was here, he began to have had doubts about moving on. This wasn't the most elegant house, but it was his, and it had served him well. He remembered the day he had first crested the mountain across the meadow and seen this place. He had been struck by its beauty, and the thought made him reluctant to leave. Also, the idea of leaving Little Raven tore at him.

Though it was still daylight, he stretched out on his buffalo robes. He was tired—tired of the killing, of the traveling, of the trouble he had brought on the Utes even though as so often happened, it had taken place when he was trying to do good.

He finally slept, but his slumber was plagued by uncomfortable dreams of dead men, the corpse of a much-abused child, the bodies of Utes ravaged by a pack of animals, and an arrow piercing his back.

He awoke in a sweat, growling in agitation as he made coffee and finished the rabbit. He still didn't know what to do. He stepped outside, figuring to enjoy the sunlight and warmth. There would be little of the latter within the next few weeks. Then he noticed half a dozen riders heading toward him fast. While he could not see who they were at this distance, they did not appear to be coming to give him a warm greeting. "This doesn't look good," he mumbled. He figured they had come from Skeeter Creek, but he had no idea how they had decided he was the one who had caused the havoc in the town or how they had found him.

Pike went back inside and got his Winchester, which would be a better weapon than his sniper rifle, he figured, and made sure it was loaded, then went back outside. When the riders were about a hundred and fifty yards away, Pike fired a warning shot. He still wasn't sure they were coming for him, and he didn't want to shoot an innocent man.

The riders slowed, then stopped. Pike leaned the rifle against the house, cupped his hands around his mouth, and bellowed, "If you boys're lookin' for trouble, you'll find it here, and you might not like it! If you ain't, ride off in some other direction!"

The response was a couple of bullets fired toward him, though they went well wide of the mark.

"Hell and damnation," Pike muttered. He picked up the Winchester, leaned against the wall for support, and fired. One of the riders fell off his horse. Pike fired again, but the men were now zigzagging, so he wasn't sure if he had hit anyone. If he had, it wasn't a fatal wound.

The attackers began firing pistols at him now that they were a lot closer. Pike fired once more and hit one of the riders, but the man did not fall. He ducked inside as bullets thudded into the wall.

Still firing, the riders raced past the house, then turned and did so again. Pike tore off the oiled paper covering one window and shot another attacker dead off his horse. The horsemen rode away from him and took shelter behind the pines that dotted the meadow.

A fusillade erupted, most of it directed toward

that window. Pike scuttled away as bullets ripped through the window and thumped into the rear adobe wall. He got his sniper rifle, went to the other front window, peeled back a corner of the covering, and slipped the barrel out. Then he waited.

The gunfire from outside dwindled, and after a few minutes, it stopped. Pike figured they were trying to decide if they had killed him but were sensible enough not to expose themselves, though once or twice, Pike saw a man stick his head out from behind a tree to get a look at the cabin. Pike sighted on where one man had done that and was patient, and eventually, the man peeped out again. Pike fired, and the man's head exploded from the .52-caliber round.

He hurried to the other window as another fusillade poured through the window he had just left. He did not have good targets to shoot at, but the attackers had to expose themselves to fire. Pike took another shot and cursed when he was off by a bit and the bullet tore a chunk out of a tree. He ducked as more lead thumped into the thick adobe walls.

Again, the rain of lead slowed, then stopped. Pike peered out the window. His enemies were not showing themselves at all now. Pike supposed they might be smart enough to wait until nightfall, then creep up on the cabin and either throw a barrage of lead into the house or perhaps jut storm it.

Pike did not relish the idea of sitting here all day facing the occasional barrage of bullets, but there was little else he could do.

He went back to the other window and peered

out, hoping he could take another shot. It was a long time coming, but a very small target presented itself when one of the men shifted behind the tree so he could take a shot at the cabin. An instant later, he was dead with a bullet through his skull.

Moments later, two men on horseback raced away to the west. One was slumped over his horse as if wounded. Pike waited a bit, then went outside. The men were almost across the meadow and had turned southeast. He figured they were heading for the road back to Skeeter Creek. He considered trying to drop one of the two but decided against it. There had been enough carnage for one day.

He wondered what he should do about the four bodies. He wasn't going to bury them, but he didn't like the thought of leaving them to the mercy of coyotes or other scavengers. He put it out of his mind for the time being. It was clear he had to get out of here and soon. He went inside and cleaned the sniper rifle and Winchester, then began gathering the things he might need.

He put a frying pan, a mug, and the coffeepot in a sack, along with a couple of plates and some utensils. He gathered the buffalo robes and the foodstuffs he had that would last him. There were few other things too, small items that meant something to him like the beaded moccasins Little Raven had made for him. Even though he had worn them only once, discovering that he was more comfortable in boots, they were special to him.

As he loaded his belongings on the mule, he wondered where he should go. He had no desire to head northeast to Denver or south toward either Arizona Territory or New Mexico Territory whence he had come here. North or northwest would be fine, he thought. He had not heard of any towns up that way, but with winter nearing fast, moving higher into the mountains would be foolish if he did not find shelter quickly.

"Doesn't matter," he muttered as he saddled the horse. Just before mounting, he looked at the decrepit house, trying to decide whether to burn it. Then he shrugged. "Wouldn't want to leave it here for some other fool to find it."

Trouble was, he had learned in New Mexico Territory that adobe did not burn. Then, with a mischievous smile, he remembered he still had two sticks of dynamite he had taken from Peabody's store. He went inside, got a bottle half-filled with coal oil, and poured some around the room. Outside, he lit the fuse of both sticks of the explosive. He tossed one inside and the other on the roof. He leaped on his horse and with the mule in tow, rode like hell. When he was fifty yards away, the house exploded.

He watched for a few minutes with a mix of sadness and satisfaction as the remnants of furniture caught afire, sending smoke up through the collapsed roof. Then he turned his horse and, towing the mule, headed north, away from Many Winters' village and Skeeter Creek. He would go where the winds and the trail took him.

He bit back the emotion that welled up inside him. He would miss his friends Crazy Hawk and Blind

Bull, but most of all, he would miss Little Raven. It ate at him that he was unable to talk to her and tell her why he was leaving.

Several miles farther on, when he entered the low mountains that flanked the wide meadow, he stopped and looked back. He could see the thin stream of smoke from the house. He also someone heading in his direction. "Damn," he muttered.

He sat there for a bit, trying to decide what to do. He was concerned that one of the men who had attacked the cabin was coming for him, but it did not seem that way. This person was moving slowly and steadily. He could drop the man from a hundred yards or so. Trouble was, he couldn't determine who the person was or that he was a danger. And, again, he would rather not shoot an innocent man.

Though the follower was still a few hundred yards away, something seemed familiar about him. He watched as the person neared. "Well, I'll be damned," he whispered and rode slowly down the hill toward Little Raven. The woman picked up speed, galloping toward him.

"What're you doin' here?" he asked when they stopped next to each other.

"Lookin' for you."

"Why?"

"I miss you. You ain't come to village in long time. I want to see how shoulder is."

"How'd you find me?"

"I saw house all fallen in, some flames too. Horse and mule gone. I follow."

"How'd you know which way I was headin?"

"I follow tracks," she said as if he were a fool.

"Well, now that you found me, turn yourself around and head on back to your village."

"Where you go?"

"Don't know." He waved a hand in a northerly direction. "Out there someplace."

"I go too."

"No. You got no business trailin' along beside me, and you'll only be a distraction."

"You not like me no more?"

Pike hesitated before he lied, "No. So just go on back home where you belong."

"I think you lie."

"Well, I didn't, so get." He turned his horse and started riding back to the hill. *Dammit, why'd she have to do this?* he wondered. He realized she was still following him, turned and stopped. "Go home!" he yelled.

She shook her head.

"Dammit, if you don't turn around and go, I'll give you a good whuppin'."

"It be okay."

Pike shook his head. He was at a loss; he didn't know how to handle such a hardheaded woman. He had no intention of hitting her again, but he couldn't think how to get her to go back to her people. "I ain't any good for you, Raven. You comin' with me would mean a hard, unsettled life. It won't be good for you. Go on back to your village and marry some brave young warrior."

"You treat me better."

"We ain't likely to have much of a lodge for a

long time."

"That okay, too."

"But you don't have anything with you. No extra clothes or your medicines, or things you need to do a woman's work."

"You wait. I go get them."

Ah, here was an out, Pike thought. "Okay, you do that. I'll wait here for you."

"You lie again. If you not here when I come, I follow."

"Could be dangerous."

"That okay. If I die, you not care anyway."

"Yes, I will, dammit." He clamped his mouth shut, knowing he had said too much.

Little Raven smiled. "I have better idea. We go back to village together. I put up a lodge for us. You build a new place if you want a white-eyes house."

"Got it all figured out, do you?"

Her grin widened. "Yep."

Pike sat, torn between his love for her and his desire not to put her in danger.

She pulled up next to him, facing him, then reached over and gently laid a work-hardened hand on his scruffy cheek. "I not afraid when I'm with you. We be okay, live long, have many children, grow old together."

"It could be dangerous for your people. I caused the trouble that ended up with the attack on Fallen Timber's camp. I don't want to be responsible for any more hurt to your tribe. There could be real trouble if the other white-eyes find out I'm livin' with the Utes. Folks from Skeeter Creek already found me and might be back. Or send the law after me."

"We handle if time comes."

"They also might come for your people and attack again."

"My people handle that if that happens. The warriors in Winter Snows' village are much stronger than Fallen Timber's. Not easy to kill."

"You're crazier than your brother, you know that?"

"Yep." She moved her hand across his shoulder, hesitating for a moment where he had been wounded, then down until she took his hand in hers.

He hesitated. There could be a real danger to her people, and he did not want to be the cause of it again. Then he thought he and Little Raven could leave the village if things got too dangerous for the Utes.

"You gonna be this exasperatin' all the time?"

"Yep." She smiled brightly.

Pike realized then that he had lost the battle. He surrendered. "I'm still the boss," he warned.

"Yep."

He was not at all sure she was speaking the truth. "All right, then let's go home."

A LOOK AT:
COLORADO RENEGADE (COLORADO TERRITORY SERIES BOOK III)

HONOR FORCES BOUNTY HUNTER ELIAS PROSPER TO TRACK DOWN A RENEGADE UTE, NO MATTER THE COST.

Bounty hunter Elias Prosper is as tough a man as the West has produced. But as hard as he is, he has a soft spot for children and women. When a Ute named Painted Bear casts off the ways of the white man and spirits away a Ute boy and a white woman, both of whom Prosper had rescued easier, the bounty hunter ignores his wife's pleas to stay home and instead heads into the mountains to hunt down the renegade warrior.

AVAILABLE JULY 2021

ABOUT THE AUTHOR

John Legg has published more than 55 novels, all on Old West themes. Blood of the Scalphunter is his latest novel in the field of his main interest — the Rocky Mountain Fur Trade. He first wrote of the fur trade in Cheyenne Lance, his initial work.

Cheyenne Lance and Medicine Wagon were published while Legg was acquiring a B.A. in Communications and an M.S. in Journalism. Legg has continued his journalism career, and is a copy editor with The New York Times News Service.

Since his first two books, Legg has, under his own name, entertained the Western audience with many more tales of man's fight for independence on the Western frontier. In addition, he has had published several historical novels set in the Old West. Among those are War at Bent's Fort and Blood at Fort Bridger.

In addition, Legg has, under pseudonyms, contributed to the Ramseys, a series that was published by Berkley, and was the sole author of the eight books in the Saddle Tramp series for HarperPaperbacks. He also was the sole author of Wildgun, an eight-book adult Western series from Berkley/Jove. He also has published numerous articles and a nonfiction book — Shinin' Trails: A Possibles Bag of Fur Trade History — on the subject,

He is member of Western Fictioneers.

In addition, he operates JL TextWorks, an editing/critiquing service.

Made in the USA
Monee, IL
26 February 2022